I0699400

RETURN TO LIZARDVILLE

LIZARDVILLE GHOST STORIES BOOK 3

RETURN TO LIZARDVILLE

STEVE ALTIER

4 Horsemen
Publications, Inc.

Return to Lizardville
Copyright © 2025 Steve Altier. All rights reserved.

Published By: 4 Horsemen Publications, Inc.

4 Horsemen Publications, Inc.
PO Box 417
Sylva, NC 28779
4horsemenpublications.com
info@4horsemenpublications.com

Cover & Typesetting by Autumn Skye
Edited by Jen Paquette

All rights to the work within are reserved to the author and publisher. No part of this publication may be reproduced, stored in a retrieval system, or transmitted in any form or by any means, electronic, mechanical, photocopying, recording, scanning, or otherwise, except as permitted under Section 107 or 108 of the 1976 International Copyright Act, without prior written permission except in brief quotations embodied in critical articles and reviews. Please contact either the Publisher or Author to gain permission.

All characters, organizations, and events portrayed in this novel are either products of the author's imagination or are used fictitiously. No generative artificial intelligence was used in the creation of this book or its cover.

All brands, quotes, and cited work respectfully belongs to the original rights holders and bear no affiliation to the authors or publisher.

Library of Congress Control Number: 2024951589

Paperback ISBN-13: 979-8-8232-0779-9
Hardcover ISBN-13: 979-8-8232-0780-5
Audiobook ISBN-13: 979-8-8232-0782-9
Ebook ISBN-13: 979-8-8232-0781-2

DEDICATION

To Kelly Altier, I'm so proud of you.

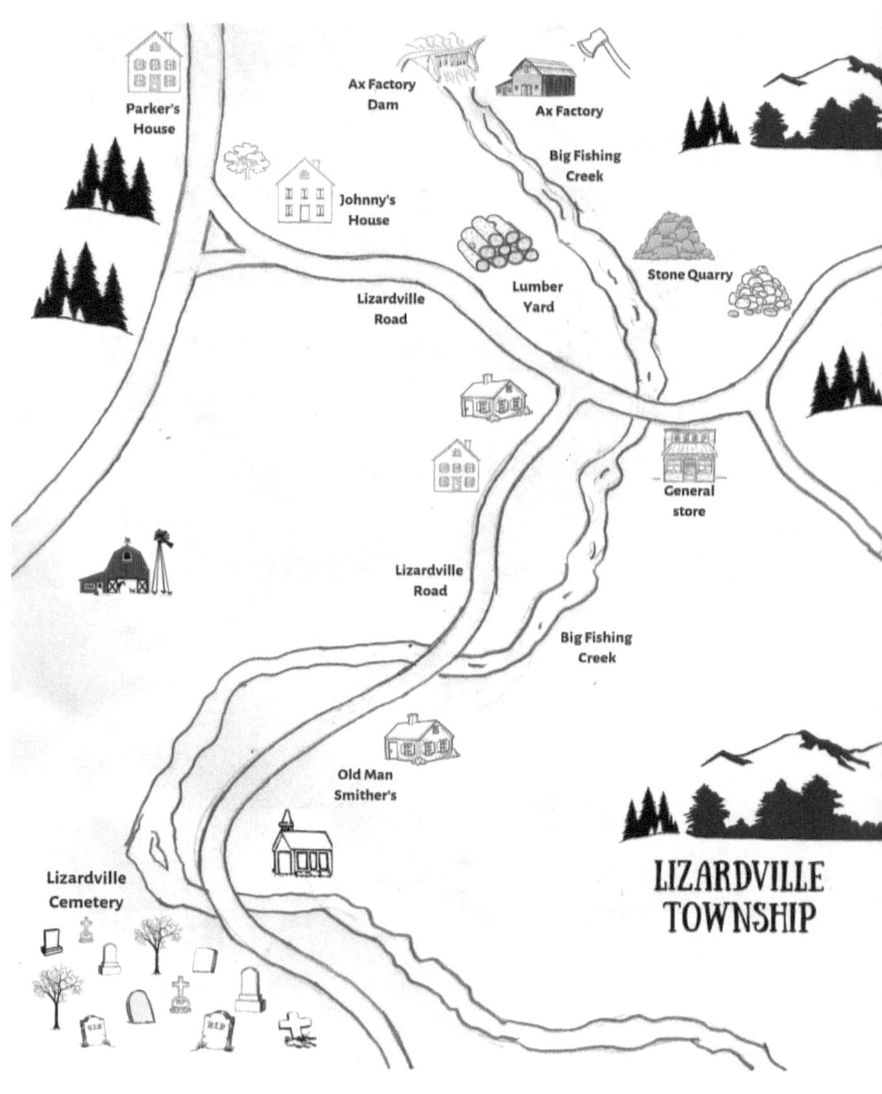
Parker's House
Ax Factory Dam
Ax Factory
Big Fishing Creek
Johnny's House
Lumber Yard
Stone Quarry
Lizardville Road
Lizardville Road
General store
Big Fishing Creek
Old Man Smither's
Lizardville Cemetery
LIZARDVILLE TOWNSHIP

CONTENTS

JOHN

ONE

Since the letter arrived, my nights have been plagued with relentless nightmares. I know it's been thirty-five years since Jimmy lost his life. Now they want me to return. Losing a friend when you're a child is something that will scar you forever. The memories refuse to fade. The image of Jimmy disappearing over the falls, the raft splitting in two, is etched in my mind. The haunting sound of the raft breaking echoes in my dreams, along with Jimmy's desperate cries for help. But it's the look of betrayal on his face as he slips beneath the water that torments me the most. Was it a final goodbye or a plea for salvation?

I woke in a cold sweat, stepped out of bed, tiptoed past the cat, and made my way to the guest room. If I couldn't sleep, the last thing I wanted to do was wake Sara. We both had to work in the morning. It might as well be me who had a rough day. Sara was the one good thing that happened in my life. Well, I can't forget my boys, Zack and Daniel. Okay, I have a lot to be thankful for. Being grateful doesn't help me sleep.

I pulled back the covers and snuggled into bed. The night was quiet, sometimes too quiet. I stared at the ceiling, unsure how that would help me sleep. *I've been to counseling as a child and even as an adult. I've done everything they ask and then some, but it can't rid my mind of the sounds and images. How could they invite me back? Yes, I've been home a time or two for a day to say hello and then return to the city Sara and I call home. Most of the time, the family gathers here.*

This time, everything is different. The family wants us to stay for an entire week for a family reunion with many activities. Lexi, Sara's older sister, was pushing this on everyone. It's not like I didn't want to pay for a hotel. We could afford it; I was using it more as an excuse. Then Lexi called Sara and agreed we could stay at her new place. She purchased a nice place out in the country. I was looking forward to seeing her home. She said she had one extra bedroom since her daughter Claire was coming into town and would occupy the other guest room. Since he had plenty of rooms, Zack and Daniel would stay at Bobby Parker's house. He had one open room, but I knew I didn't want to sleep in that house. I don't think I would ever be able to sleep knowing Jimmy could appear at any moment. Parker was Sara's older brother by three years. I'm unsure how I felt about my boys staying in a haunted house. They always wanted to stay there, but you know the old saying, be careful what you wish for.

My older brother Buck lived in our old house with Mom and Dad. It would be great to see them again. Buck said his son Ryan was also going to be there. How was I going to survive the week? My therapist said this would be good for me, that I needed to face my fears. The one thing I never told my doctor was that my fear was still alive. Well, if you count a ghost as alive.

I hadn't seen Jimmy since the day after we put Annabelle and Donald Thornhill to rest at the old cemetery. Jimmy broke his promise. I'm not sure what his motives were. That never sat well with me. I'm sure Jimmy still looks the same. He died when he was thirteen. I bet he's still wearing those cutoff corduroy shorts; they were his favorite. But they are so out of style now. Like he was ever worried about style. I laughed at my joke.

What if he appears? How will he feel about Sara and me? Will he think we abandoned him? After high school, we decided to get a fresh start. We moved to the city of brotherly love. Yes, Philadelphia. We shared a small apartment for many years and then finally purchased a townhome. Fifteen years ago, we could afford a nice place an hour outside the city. Sara found an excellent job at a local medical clinic only a few miles from the house. I worked from home, writing articles for local papers and publishing a book or two a year.

Sara hounds me about writing our childhood stories. She thinks it would be a great series of books. I've mentioned a few things in other stories, but I'm not sure I was ready to disclose all the details of my childhood to the world. Maybe one day soon but back to the real problem. I am returning to Lizardville after all these years.

Zack and Daniel were bringing their girlfriends on this trip, and that's all I needed: to be responsible for two more lives. There's nothing like adding more pressure on me. The door inched open. I froze, and my heart rate increased. I leaned forward. The air conditioner didn't turn on, and the doors didn't open alone. I looked around and didn't see anything. My fingers twitched, a nervous habit I have when I get excited. I laid my head on the pillow and pulled the cover over my head. *What am I, ten?* I slowly lowered the blanket past my eyes and then my mouth. I gazed around. The room was empty, just me and four walls. My breathing was heavy. I need to get this under control. "Crap," I yelled when the cat lunged into bed and cuddled at my feet. If I kept this up, I would have a heart attack and wouldn't need to worry about facing Jimmy. I stared at the ceiling a bit longer.

"John." Sara nudged me. "Hey, it's time to wake up." I opened my eyes to see her smile. "Thanks." I smiled back. That's the best way to start the day.

"I'm heading out," Sara said, turning for the door. She didn't have to ask why I was in the guest room. She already figured it out. "Oh, John, I'll be home early, so please get the luggage down from the attic because we need to pack," she said from the doorway before leaving.

"No problem." I hope she heard me as she walked away. That's what I needed to do today: get in the attic. That reminds me of the last time I was in an attic back home. Things didn't go so well. *Let's hope today will be different.*

I pushed the covers to the side and forced myself to get out of bed. *Maybe I'll get a little writing done, then take a nap.* Now, that was a plan. After I showered and had my breakfast, I sat down to finish a bit of writing. I wrote a thousand words in my new novel—*The Basket Maker Hallows*. Before laying down for a quick power nap, I thought pulling down the luggage first was best. I didn't want to forget that.

I walked slowly toward the garage; it was times like this that I missed the attic in my bedroom. It was a typical door and staircase that led to the attic. It had a complete floor, and I could stand up, but I was shorter back then. I was only a kid.

I opened the interior garage door and stared at the ceiling. I was not too fond of this pull-down attic door because I always felt like I would fall on the steep stairs, or they would break. I raised my hand slightly, wrapped two shaking hands around the white cord, and pulled. It felt stuck, so I pulled again, and the door finally gave way. I extended my hands over my head and pulled the ladder down until it touched the floor. I also made sure the anti-slip device was locked in place.

I hesitated; my heart thumped in my chest. I don't know why I was nervous. I'd been in the attic twenty or thirty times since we lived here. There was nothing to be afraid of. This was not the attic back home. I smiled. *I am being silly*. I placed my foot on the first rung, then the other foot on the second rung, and began my climb. If I remembered correctly, the luggage was on the left-hand side. I could grab it and go.

Just another step before I reached the top. I inched my way upward and peeked over the opening. It was dark. I should have brought a flashlight. I took another step, placed my hands on the floor, and pulled myself up until I could stand. I waved my hand around, searching for the pull-down cord until I found it, and then tugged at it. The light flicked on, and I could see everything was normal. There were no ghosts here. I looked left and then right. I located the luggage at the far end of the attic. I found that odd. I never put it over there. I moved my foot forward to the sound of a creaking board. I froze. A shiver ran down my spine. *Stop being silly. Everything is fine.* This whole trip had me on edge.

I slowly moved my right foot and then my left. I inched my way across the attic floor. The wind howled outside, and a draft of wind rushed through the vents. It sent a shiver down my spine. *For goodness sake, you're a grown man; pull yourself together, John.* I stared at the luggage: three bags. I had better bring them all down, or Sara would send me back up for the one I left behind. I took a deep breath and another step. I reached down and grabbed the handle of the enormous bag. Picking it up, I glanced around again and turned to face the attic door. I walked briskly over, set the bag next to the opening, then spun, and walked back to grab the smaller two bags. *See, there is nothing to be afraid of.* I reached down as another gust of wind raced through the attic. *I don't remember them talking about any storms rolling in.* I bent over and then straightened.

My fingers trembled. I rubbed my chin and inhaled. I bent over and grabbed the first of the smaller bags. *See, there's nothing to worry about.* I leaned over, wrapping my hand around the second handle, and my right hand began to itch. I trembled as the itch continued to my wrist. I glanced downward, dropped both bags, and swatted the spider off my arm. "Crap." I shook all over, my arms flailing at my sides. I jumped back. I raised my right foot over the spider and noticed it was only a daddy longlegs. I remember watching a television show one afternoon about spiders, and they said the daddy longlegs spider doesn't have a venom gland or fangs. They pose no threat to people. *That's not what I've always heard. I remember pulling out my phone and fact-checking the show on Google, and they were correct.* I did find it odd for the spider to be in my attic. They were commonly found in the cellar. Another interesting fact is they don't spin webs because they don't produce silk. That is why I didn't notice him. If I had seen a web, I would have been more careful where I placed my hands. I lowered my foot to the side of the spider and watched him scurry away.

I inhaled and then exhaled, trying to lower my heart-rate. Quickly, I grabbed both handles, one with each hand, spun, and briskly walked to the attic door. I set them down and turned around, placing one foot on the stairs. I grabbed the first bag, quickly went down, and set it on the garage floor. I repeated this process twice, folded the ladder up, and closed the door, catching a glimpse of the light as it closed. *Dang it.*

I grabbed the cord, pulled the door, lowered the ladder in frustration, climbed back to the top, and paused. It was freezing up here. How could the temperature change so quickly? Something moved like a blur in the wind out of the corner of my eye. We have lived here long enough for me to know we don't have ghosts in our house. I was pretty sure of it; maybe it was a raccoon or squirrel. But that didn't explain the chill in the air. We've lived in this house for over fifteen years, and I've never noticed anything odd in the past. It must be my mind playing tricks on me. The trip to Lizardville had me spooked. I shook my head. *It's all in your mind.* I'd deal with it when we get home. Right now, I just wanted to leave the attic. I stood up, reached, and pulled the cord. Now, the only light came from the garage. I turned and started down the ladder, pausing one last time, and glanced around. Yes, I was positive my mind was playing tricks on me. I descended, stepped on the floor, folded the ladder, and let the door slam.

I grabbed one of the towels from my workbench and wiped off the luggage before bringing it into the house. I carried them to the bedroom and laid them on the bed. I decided not to tell Sara about the spider, something moving, or the attic's chill—no reason for her to worry. I'd call an exterminator when we get home. Now, it was time for that nap.

TWO

I woke to the sound of the garage door opening. Sara was home, and my mind raced. Had I done everything she asked? I wouldn't say I like to disappoint her. That wasn't how I wanted to start this trip. I sat up and went to the kitchen to check the sink. The dishes were done. I breathed a sigh of relief. The door opened. "I'm home," Sara hollered.

"I'm in the kitchen," I said.

"Did you, by chance, get the tent out of the attic?"

"No, but I got the luggage," I replied, a bit puzzled. This was new. *Why do we need a tent?*

"Zack called. He, his brother, and the girls are going to camp out at Lexi's," she said as she entered the kitchen.

"I'll get the tent out of the attic." I smiled and returned to the garage. When I opened the door, I hoped that whatever was up there had left. I stood, pulled the light, and grabbed the box labeled "family tent." I lowered the box to the garage floor, returned, pulled the cord, and closed the attic. *Not so bad this time.*

"Got it," I hollered to the bedroom.

"Why haven't you packed? The kids are already on the way. We need to get on the road," Sara said.

"I thought we were leaving tomorrow morning." *Why am I always the last to know things?*

"Sorry. Change of plans." Sara smiled and laughed. She was excited to see her family; the boys must be excited about visiting Lizardville. *Boy, won't they be disappointed? There isn't much to do there.*

I opened my suitcase and then the drawer on the chest of drawers. I started grabbing socks, underwear, t-shirts, and a few pairs of shorts. I walked to the closet and picked out a few nice shirts and a couple of pairs of jeans. I even tossed a jacket in the bag just in case. I walked to the bathroom, picked up my overnight toiletry bag, and glanced in to take inventory. Everything seemed to be in order. I stuffed it in my suitcase and zipped it up. "Done," I said and shot Sara a smug look.

"Thank you." She smiled. She was ignoring my smirk. "You can take this one to the car." She pointed to the large bag in the corner. I grabbed mine and hers, walked to the garage, and opened the hatch on our SUV. I placed the two bags inside, picked up the tent box, and then dusted it off before sliding it into the back. I thought about the sleeping bags. I darted to the hall closet, grabbing four of them in case the boys or their girlfriends forgot. I stuffed them in the back and closed the hatch.

"Are we going to take a cooler?" Sara asked from the doorway. She startled me.

"Um, just a small one for the trip. Does that sound good?"

"No, bring the large one, so we have room for whatever we need," Sara said, closing the door behind her.

I grabbed the large ice chest, placing a dozen canned sodas inside. Then, I added a small milk, a few ice packs, and a half bag of ice. She would add more items, but I placed the cooler in the back seat anyway. I noticed the small piece of luggage next to the door. I scooped it up, putting it in the rear of the car. I thought we had everything. I wondered if the kids were riding with us or if they would follow us. *Why would they want to ride in the car with Dad?* I chuckled at the thought.

I walked back to the kitchen. "The car's packed." I leaned forward, kissing Sara softly.

She said, "I'm ready. The boys should be along any minute."

That was music to my ears. *Let's get this trip started.* I only wished for an uneventful vacation. It was about a three-hour drive to Lizardville. I hate to admit it, but seeing the old gang, my parents, and, okay, even my brother would be pretty cool.

I heard brakes squeal out front. *I thought Zack was going to get them fixed.* Sara bounced up and down. I hadn't seen her this excited for some time. The boys were together, and they had their girlfriends with them. Zack pushed the front door open; Sara mugged him before he could say hello. He was followed by Daniel and two girls whom I recognized from a previous visit.

"That's why I always let Zack go first." Daniel pointed to his brother, still smothered by Sara. "Dad, you remember Beth," Daniel said.

"Of course. It's good to see you again." Beth gave me a quick hug. She was friendly, about twenty-one, a slim brunette with curly hair about shoulder length. She was 5'2".

She seemed the perfect match for Daniel as he was a little taller than her.

Sara finally moved from Zack and cornered Daniel, who gave me a look. *Save me!* Zack stepped forward to say hello with a quick hug, followed by a quick hug and hello from Amy, who was twenty-three, slim, with long blonde hair and a quirky personality that was the perfect fit for Zack. "I thought you were going to get your brakes fixed?" I glared at Zack.

"I know. I just haven't had time." Zack paused. "I'll take care of them when we get back. Or maybe Uncle Parker can take a look at them?" he added.

"I told him you would mention it." Amy tapped me on the arm. "But what do I know?" She gave a slight giggle.

"Don't feel bad. He doesn't listen to me either." I gave Zack a sarcastic smile. "Alright, we had better get on the road, or you four will be setting up the tent in the dark." I laughed, and Sara shot me this cute little smile.

"Oh, I almost forgot. You know what I say. Never pass on an opportunity to use the bathroom. So, do it now because we are not stopping," I said firmly. The looks I received were not the best, but it didn't faze me. However, I did notice that Beth and Amy darted to the bathroom. I was proud of them.

I slowed the car, taking the Salona exit off Interstate 80. I quickly realized nothing had changed in the area. Back in Philly, there was new construction happening daily. Suddenly, I felt like a child again—that nervous kid who was unsure of himself. I slowed my pace and glanced in the rearview mirror. Zack was only a few car lengths behind.

The interstate changed our area a little. It made the trip more accessible, yet many cars would drive past with no reason to stop. That meant less money for the area. I pulled onto Salona Road. I flashed back to my childhood. The fire station hadn't changed, except maybe a new coat of paint. Fishing Creek still looked the same with the mountains and a few farms scattered here and there.

I paused at the next stop sign, glancing at the road sign: Lizardville Road. A shiver ran down my spine when a male voice whispered in my ear, "*Turn back.*" I abruptly pulled off the road. My breathing was heavy, my heart pounding and my stomach tied in knots.

"Are you alright?" Sara asked.

That couldn't be Donald Thornhill. We crossed him over a long time ago. It wasn't Jimmy's voice. He was still a teenager. *So, who was that?*

"John," Sara yelled and nudged me. "Are you alright? You're scaring me," Sara repeated.

"Dad, you alright?" Zack said, tapping on the driver's side window.

"John, you are pale and clammy. Please answer me," Sara insisted. I felt her hand on my cheek and then my throat. I turned to face her.

"Did you hear the warning?" My heart raced.

Sara leaned over me and unlocked my door; Zack opened it. "Dad, are you alright?" I nodded.

"John, what's going on? Talk to me." Sara's hand felt soft on my arm as she rubbed back and forth. "Do we need to go to the hospital?"

"Did you hear the voice?" I leaned over and whispered to Sara. I did not want to alarm Zack.

"What voice?" Sara returned my whisper.

"He said, 'Turn back.' It was a warning from a male voice." I was starting to feel better. Just a little startled. *How could his voice have entered my car to give me a warning?* "I'm fine, only antsy," I replied. I glanced at my hand. My fingers were twitching again.

"Dad, is this about the stories you told us when we were kids?" Zack asked. His expression was puzzled. I nodded. "Dad, they are just stories, pages in your novel, but they are not real," Zack assured me as he patted me on the shoulder. "You're gonna be fine, Pops," Zack snickered and returned to his car.

He pulled alongside my car. "See you at Uncle Parker's house," Zack hollered.

I nodded. Sara continued to stare at me. "What?" I asked.

"I'm worried about you, John." Her lips grazed my cheek. I smiled, pulled the car out of the driveway, and followed Zack to Parker's house. Moments later, I pulled alongside Zack's car in the driveway. Everyone was outside greeting Parker. Sara jumped out and dashed to her brother. I spotted Buck mingling with everyone. But I needed a moment to myself. The voice puzzled me to no end. *Why the warning? Who was it from? Why did the voice sound familiar?* This was going to drive me crazy. *Should I warn the others? Sara, Buck, and Parker? How could Sara and I, upon returning to Lizardville, wake up the spirit world? I need help mentally.*

The car door burst open, and Buck grabbed my arm, yanking me out of the car. "What's up, little brother?" Buck questioned as he tried to put me in a headlock.

"We're not kids anymore," I said, shoving him off me. "I'm good, and how are you?"

"I'm good. It's fun living with Mom and Dad again," Buck said in a sarcastic tone.

"I'm sure it is," I replied, not wanting to get into details.

"They want you, Sara, and the boys to swing by before going to Lexi's, alright?"

"We don't have much time before the sun goes down, and the boys want to pitch the tent out at Lexi's. Tell them we will swing by tomorrow." I smiled, and Buck nodded.

I turned to face Sara and the boys. I noticed the boys were both staring at the dam and remnants of the factory. I snapped my finger a few times and told them we had to hustle if they wanted to get the tent pitched tonight. Parker and Buck decided to tag along, and I was okay with that.

"Where's Lexi's new house?" I asked.

"Follow me," Parker said as he and Buck climbed into his black pickup truck. I opened the door for Sara and helped her into the car. I walked to the driver's side, opened my door, and fastened my seat belt. I turned the key, put the car in reverse, and followed Parker's pickup down Lizardville Road. I checked my mirror to make sure the boys were behind me.

We drove past the house where I grew up. Zack blew his horn as we drove by. I'm not sure Mom and Dad heard him. I'd call them when we got to Lexi's house. We continued by the lumberyard. I noticed it had doubled in size. I guessed business had been good for them. We turned right on Lizardville Road before Big Fishing Creek and the General Store, where I had my first job. I forgot to ask if Tom still owned the place. I would guess he sold it and retired. I wondered if he was still alive. Who owned it now, and would they know who I was? It's funny how time flies, and you lose track of old friends.

I glanced out over the creek. It always looked peaceful. It was times like that that I missed my childhood. I slowed the car, enjoying the scenery. I missed my days on the water; fishing and camping were two of my favorite things. I hadn't been fishing in years, not since the boys grew up and moved out. Maybe we could get a little fishing in while we were here. That would be a blast.

"Turn around and go home," the male voice whispered. I jerked the wheel to the right and then left. Sara screamed, and I straightened up the car.

"What on earth are you doing?" Sara yelled, her hands trembling.

"Sorry, I heard the voice again, which freaked me out. He told me to turn around and go home. I should know this voice, but I can't pinpoint it yet," I explained to Sara, who was staring at me like I was crazy.

"I think you are worrying about nothing," Sara said.

I was sure she was right. I'd built up most of this in my head. Obviously, I didn't want to come home for the week. I'd been on vacation before with no issues. Yet, on this vacation, I was hearing voices in my head.

We went over the old bridge that we used to jump off and swim when we rafted down the creek. This was always one of my favorite places. I remember that day when Jimmy jumped off the top rail of the bridge. He got stuck underwater and told me about his crazy puzzle box story. I didn't believe him then, but I sure do now.

Parker used his right turn signal. I freaked out for a moment, as did Sara. Why were we turning down Old Man Smithers' driveway? He rounded the corner and vanished in the brush. I followed suit and turned right. I passed the tree line, and the yard opened into a large clearing. I noticed a small house sitting next to the river. It had a fresh coat of paint on it and lots of flowers around the front. Lexi and her daughter Claire were waiting to greet us.

"Did you know she bought Old Man Smithers' house?" I said sharply.

"I did not." Sara gave me this bizarre look.

"I don't want to stay here," I begged.

"I think we will be alright. After all, Lexi is living here. Let's give it a night, please." Sara gave me that sad look, and I melted.

"One night, but if anything happens, I'm out of here," I said.

"We'll be fine." Sara smiled. The car stopped, and Sara was out the door, hugging her sister quicker than I could say no.

THREE

Staying at Old Man Smithers' house was not what I expected. I wasn't sure I could stay there. I didn't have any fond memories of the place, only bad ones. I could tell by Sara's reaction that this came as a surprise to her, too. I sat momentarily, watching Zack, Daniel, and the girls meet in the yard. They had no idea whose house this was. *Why would Lexi buy Old Man Smithers' house? She must have lost her mind. Was it revenge?* I knew the house was secluded and had lots of land. But I still would not have bought this house. I'd be sure to ask her why.

My fingers twitched as I tried opening my door. I stepped out and approached my family who were gathered on the lawn. The boys had already unloaded their car and pulled the tent and sleeping bags from the back of mine. I walked up behind Sara and gave her a nudge.

"You remember Claire?" Sara said. She was pointing to our niece.

"Wow, the last time I saw you, you were like this tall." I held my hand out a little above my waist.

"Uncle John, we all grow up. It's been a long time since we have seen you," Claire said, and I nodded. "So, how is the writing going? Any bestsellers?" Claire asked.

"I've had some success, but I'm enjoying the journey," I responded and smiled. "Congratulations on becoming a Registered Nurse. I see you are following the ladies in the family. Your mom and Sara are both nurses. I'm proud of you," I said and hugged her quickly.

Lexi strolled up and hugged me. She always liked me because I cared for her sister; we had all been through so much as kids. When you go through something as a group, it strengthens friendships.

"How have you been, Lexi?" I asked quizzically.

"I'm fine." She gave me this odd stare. "I know. Why did I buy this house?" Lexi added.

"Dang, girl. Now you can read minds?" I said and chuckled.

"I'm sure it was on your mind," Lexi said. "Well," she grinned, "I love the location; it has so much potential."

"The place looks better than I remember," I said.

"When I heard Mr. Smithers passed away, I drove here to look around. By chance, Terry, the realtor, was here looking around. So, he gave me a tour," Lexi said, spreading her hands to show off her home.

"But the history?" I asked.

"What history?"

"You know, the bad blood between him and us." I gave her a wry smile.

"If I remember, he had an issue with you boys, not me." Lexi furrowed her eyebrows.

"Um, I guess you have a valid point," I said. *She was right. He didn't like us boys, yet he did help us when we needed him most. Come to think of it, we didn't see much of him after that day in the cemetery. I wonder why?* I gazed over Lexi's shoulder and watched Zack, Daniel, Amy, and Beth work together to erect the tent as a team. I almost forgot how big the thing was. Yes, there would be plenty of room for the four of them.

Lexi snapped her finger at me, pulling my attention back to her as Sara walked over. They entered the house, and I grabbed our luggage from behind the car. After making a few trips, I paused to reflect on how pretty it was. The bluffs cascaded upward into the mountains on the far side of the river—the gentle flow of water soothing with light ripples as the stream flowed by. A calmness flooded my body. I was starting to get a better feeling. This week was going to be fun.

After the tent was up, the boys set up the horseshoes. Buck and Parker lost several times as Sara, Lexi, and I sat watching from the screened porch. The sun dipped below the tree line, casting darkness on the lawn. The boys piled a few logs on the fire, and I watched it roar to life.

We grabbed our lawn chairs, forming a circle around the fire. "Does anyone have marshmallows?" Sara asked.

"No, but you could pass me a beer."

Buck opened the cooler, handing Lexi a nice cold one.

Parker pulled up a chair next to Claire, Beth, and Amy. "Would you like to hear a ghost story?" he asked.

"No," Sara and Lexi screamed in unison.

"Come on. You know they're gone," Parker said with an evil grin.

"Come on, man. The ladies said no. Besides, Jimmy's still around," I said.

"You act like these stories are real?" Amy chimed in. "Daniel and Zack told us all about them. Nothing happened." Amy gave me a look of disbelief.

"Amy's right. Nothing happened when they told us the story," Beth added. "Come on, Mr. Malone, tell us."

"Please call me John, and for the last time, no, you don't understand." My voice elevated, and my hand started to twitch. Sara noticed and laid her hand on mine. I took a deep breath. "The last time Parker told this story, I was thirteen. I spent over a year running for my life. I also lost my best friend." I broke out in a sweat. My spine tingled. "News flash for you all: this is not a game you want to play. It comes down to life or death." I pushed my chair back, waved my hand, and walked to the house to escape this nonsense. The last thing we needed was to wake up the spirit world.

"Dude, come on back," Parker yelled. I kept walking. I wanted no part of this.

Buck grabbed my arm, pulling me backward. "Johnny, it's alright. Parker and I tell the stories all the time. Nothing happens. They're gone, don't you get it?"

"What if you're wrong?" I snapped, the words escaping me before I could reconsider. One question echoed in my mind: *What about the persistent voice I've been hearing?* As I looked up, the night sky stretched before me, clear and vast, stars twinkling like distant beacons. The soft murmur of the nearby creek reached my ears, its gentle flow soothing my thoughts. Around me, crickets chirped in a symphony while sporadic bursts of light from lightning bugs danced in the darkness.

"You're my brother, and I wouldn't put you in harm's way. Besides, we're adults now, and they're not kids." Buck pointed to my boys. I had never heard Buck this passionate about anything. I looked toward Sara; she raised her arms to her side. She was as confused as I was. Buck glanced upward. "It's a pretty night. Nothing is going to happen."

"I sure hope you're right," I said, laying my arm over his shoulder and walking back to the fire. Daniel, Zack, and the others nodded. I guessed they wanted to do this. The fire crackled, sending a few sparks into the night sky.

"It's different when you tell a story about an area when you are hundreds of miles away. Tonight, you're sitting where the events took place," I said, making eye contact with each of them. The girls smiled, as did Zack and Daniel. My gut told me not to tempt fate. I sure hoped I was wrong about this.

"Alright," Parker said as he rubbed his hands together. He couldn't wait to share his story with everyone. I felt Sara's soft touch on my arm. I half smiled, sat quietly, and listened as Parker reminisced.

Clouds rolled in, covering the moon. An ominous feeling rushed over me. I couldn't hear the crickets anymore. I gazed at the others; Parker had them in a trance with his story. They sat on the edge of their seats. They were glued to his every word. I gripped the armrest until my knuckles turned white. "Relax," Sara whispered in my ear.

"You were not there when Parker told this story thirty-five years ago. I was, and from that night on, all hell broke loose," I whispered in Sara's ear. She rubbed my arm, trying to comfort me. It wasn't working.

An hour passed, Parker finished his story, the kids asked tons of questions, and he told them the truth. Even though Daniel and Zack heard this from me years ago, I still didn't think they believed any of it. I wanted it to stay that way.

The party broke up, and it was finally time to get some sleep. I was exhausted from the drive and the events of the day. I knew I would sleep like a log, or I hoped I would.

FOUR

Jimmy's hand slipped under the water, and I reached out and tried to pull him out. I couldn't. I lunged forward. My body was hot and clammy. I looked to my left. Sara was still asleep. It was a dream, more like a nightmare, the same one I'd had ever since the invitation arrived. I touched my phone: 3:30. Today was going to be a long day. I needed sleep. We had to go over early to help Parker set up for the family reunion. I didn't want to go inside his house, but I didn't have a choice.

I forced myself out of bed. I needed to use the bathroom if I wanted to go back to sleep. I pushed the hallway bathroom door. I used the moonlight to see and did what I came to do.

"Get out."

I froze, letting the water run in the sink. I looked right, left, and even behind me. *Nothing!* I washed my hands, turned off the water, and returned to bed.

"Get out," a man said.

I knew I was awake. This was not a dream. My hands were still cold from the water. I walked down the hallway to the living room and glanced around at an empty room. I must be losing my mind. I turned.

"*Get out!*" the man's voice yelled.

How can Sara sleep through this? I had to be half asleep. I forced myself to go back to bed and ignored the warnings. I slid under the covers and pulled them over my head. I knew this would not protect me. I felt foolish, but it gave me comfort.

The noise of water running and sunlight beaming through the curtains caught my attention. I was a bit startled when I noticed it was already 7:30. I sat up, stretched, and went to the bathroom where Sara was showering.

"Why did ya let me sleep so late?" I asked.

"Hi, I thought you needed more sleep." Sara smiled and turned off the water. "I'm done if you want to get in. I can finish in the bedroom." She wrapped the towel around her body.

"Sure, why not?" *I hope there is still hot water.* I did what I needed to, and about thirty minutes later, I left the bathroom feeling like a new man.

I met the others in the kitchen, grabbed a bite to eat, and then helped everyone load things in the car. It would have been better to have the reunion here at Lexi's instead of Parkers'. But this was not my call. I grabbed a box of food and loaded it in the rear of my SUV. Zack, Daniel, and the girls were ready to take off. I grabbed the boys and asked them for one favor: Please stay away from the dam. They promised.

I watched as they drove out of sight. "Are you going to help?" Sara chuckled and wrapped her arms around my waist.

"Do you ever get weird feelings?" I said over my shoulder.

"What do you mean, like this moment?"

"No." I paused, unsure if I should tell her. But we didn't keep secrets from each other—the key to a good relationship. "I heard a voice last night telling me to leave this place." I gazed over my shoulder and noticed the smirk on Sara's face. "Now I feel like something bad is going to happen today."

"Oh, John," Sara squeezed me, "you are overthinking this. These feelings started the day the letter arrived. Relax and try to have some fun. Please, for me." Sara nibbled on my ear. She knew how to win me over. Sara was right. *I need to relax. I'm going to see Mom and Dad in a bit, and I heard a surprise guest or two is expected.*

"What else do we need to load up?" I asked.

"That's my big boy." Sara patted my chest and pointed at a few more boxes of food and snacks.

I grabbed them and loaded the car. Lexi and Claire gave us a wave and pulled away. I opened the car door for Sara, then walked to the driver's side, and climbed in.

The drive was peaceful. I didn't miss the traffic jams in Philly. I don't think we spotted one car on the road. Nothing had changed. I pulled into Parker's front yard. There were a dozen cars lined up. The boys ran out along with Buck and Parker to help unload the vehicle.

This place brought back memories. *Spooky times in the attic, playing games in the basement. Those were good times.* I grabbed the last box and followed Sara around the side of the house. Parker had done a great job of setting this up. Mom and Dad sat beside Sara's parents at the first picnic table. We set our boxes down and greeted them with hugs and kisses. My parents had aged but still looked fantastic for a couple in their seventies.

Four picnic tables were lined up in a row, two covered in food. We had enough food to feed an army. Parker stood over a large grill while Buck stood next to the other. I have a hard time cooking on one normal-sized grill. I watched Parker flip the hamburgers. When he opened the lid on the second grill, smoke rolled out. Were we sending smoke signals to the ghosts?

I sat beside Sara, gazed over, and observed my boys interacting with Amy and Beth. They beamed, and that made me smile. I loved to see them so happy. Ryan arrived. That was Buck's son. *Gee, I haven't seen him in a few years. Man, has he grown?* He was a year older than Zack and slightly taller.

The reunion was in full swing. I sat and chatted with Mom and Dad for an hour and then spent about as much time with Sara's parents. We made plans to spend tomorrow with the four of them and have dinner together. One of Parker's surprises was Stewart. He stopped by. I called him Scooter as a kid, and much to my surprise, he preferred Scooter.

I spent the next two hours catching up with Scooter, and he told me Todd had moved away after high school. It would have been nice to see him. Scooter said his goodbyes, and I walked him to the car. It was great catching up. There were fewer cars here than when we arrived. Seeing some of Sara's aunts, uncles, and cousins was great. The day had turned out to be a success.

I walked to the rear of the house and spotted Sara chatting with Lexi. The two were extremely close, especially after that summer in 1976. We all were close. I gave them a nod as I approached.

"Have you seen Zack or Daniel?" I asked.

"No, I'm sure they're in the house with the younger crowd." Sara smiled. I turned to find the boys. "John?" she asked.

"Yes?" I spun around.

"Are you glad we came?"

"Of course I am." I grinned. "Thank you." I walked inside the house. Yes, I was glad we came. It was great seeing everyone and catching up. We might have to do this more often. I pushed the back door open and walked into an empty kitchen. I strolled to the living room. It, too, was empty. I walked downstairs to the basement. It, too, was silent. I walked upstairs. *Gosh, it's been years since I was up here*. I flashed back to my childhood. Lexi and Sara's room looked the same. *Dang, they haven't changed anything*. I opened and closed each door. That left one place for the boys to hide. I paused for a second and then opened the attic door. I remembered the séance we held up here. A shiver ran down my spine. The attic was dark. I pulled the string, and the light flicked on. I looked to the right and then left. The room was empty. I walked to the far side and gazed out the small window.

The city and county had worked together to reshape and remove half the dam. The water flowed by at a peaceful, slow pace around the far side. The walkway remained halfway and served as a fishing pier. But my boys were not there. My stomach turned.

"*You were warned*!" a voice said.

I turned around quickly. I was alone. My heart thumped in my chest. I dropped to one knee. I was gasping for breath. *Not my kids!*

I stood, scrambled to the stairs, and dashed into Sara's bedroom. I pulled the curtains back, looked over the backyard, and spotted my parents and Sara's. Buck and Parker chatted beside the grill with other aunts, uncles, and a few minor children playing in the yard. Sara and Lexi were still sitting at the picnic table with our parents. I couldn't locate Zack, Daniel, or Ryan. No, Amy, Beth, or Claire either. My heart sank, and my knees went weak. I stumbled to the floor. *This can't happen; please tell me they are not missing*. I placed my hand on the wall to help me reach my feet.

I knew this wasn't a good idea. I told Sara this from the start. But no one ever listened to me. I stared out the window one last time. The boys and girls were not there. I took a deep breath, pushed off the wall, and started for the door. I stopped when I heard a noise in the attic. I stood still. There it was again. I darted to the attic door, jerked it open, and dashed up the stairs. I pulled the light on and spotted a small raccoon staring back at me. "Hi, little fellow, how did you get in here?" I didn't have time to waste on him. "I'll be sure to let Parker know you live here." I turned the light off, dashed down the stairs, and shut the door behind me.

Out the bedroom and down the main hallway, then I ran down the grand staircase. I checked all the rooms and yelled down the cellar stairs. Still no sign of any of them. *Where could they have gone?* I peeked out front, but their car remained in the same spot. I briskly walked to the back door. I paused to gather my wits. I couldn't raise any alarms. I didn't want to start a panic; I was already a mess and didn't want Sara or Lexi to freak out.

I pushed the door open and slowly walked toward Sara. She took one look at me. Her face went long, and her smile disappeared. She always had a way of reading me. Lexi noticed next and stopped mid-conversation. My parents stared at me as Sara and Lexi stood and walked toward me. I stopped dead in my tracks.

"What's wrong?" Sara placed her hands on my cheeks.

"Don't panic," I urged.

"Tell me now," Sara's voice elevated.

"The kids are missing,"

"What do you mean, missing?" Sara asked.

"We'll find them." The pain in Sara's eyes almost killed me. Buck and Parker approached.

"What's going on?" Buck asked.

I took a deep breath. "Ryan, Zack, Daniel, and the girls are missing," I said. "I called them and sent a text but no response."

"I'm sure they're around here somewhere," Parker said, his left eye twitching. "Have you looked inside?" he asked.

"Yes, top to bottom," I answered. I looked around the backyard. They were nowhere in sight.

"Buck and I will head over to the dam and look around. You three search the house, check the coal and storage room in the basement, and meet back here in ten minutes," Parker commanded.

Sara, Lexi, and I checked every room in the house; we agreed they were not there and made our way to the back-yard. Buck and Parker arrived moments later. I noticed Buck giving me a nod as they approached.

"Where could they have gone?" Sara demanded.

"It looks like we're going for a hike," Parker said as he raised his eyebrow and turned up the corner of his mouth.

"Did you tell Ryan where the cave is?" My voice was louder than expected. Sara and Lexi stared at Parker until he cracked.

"Not just me. Buck and I showed Ryan where it was located last summer," Parker said while I noticed Buck trying to shake his hands at Parker without drawing attention to himself.

"I can't believe you two," Lexi said through gritted teeth.

"Grab the gear," Sara barked at Buck and Parker. "We're going for a walk!"

ZACK

FIVE

Amy and I finished our lunch with Grandma and Grandpa. *They hit it off, and I'm sure they approved of Amy. Maybe it's time for Amy and I to start thinking about our future together. I'm sure Mom would love it.* We walked over to join Daniel and Beth just as Ryan walked up.

"It's great seeing you again, Ryan. Have you been hitting the gym?" I asked. He was always taller than me but had filled out quite well.

"So, who is this pretty lady?" Ryan smiled while he shot Amy a nod.

"This is Amy," I said as she extended her hand, ignoring his attempt to get a hug.

"Do you have a girlfriend?" Amy asked.

"Nah, no pretty ladies around here. I guess I'll have to start looking in the big city." Ryan smirked.

Amy wrapped her arm around mine, pulling me tight, and Claire joined us.

"Hi Claire, this is Amy." I pointed.

"It's a pleasure to meet you and ignore anything this idiot has to say. I learned the hard way." Claire rolled her eyes at Ryan.

"Have you guys ever walked on the dam?" Ryan asked, changing the subject.

"No, Dad always told us to stay off the dam," I responded.

"Really, you still listen to your daddy?" Ryan chuckled. "How about you, Daniel? Do you and Beth want to see it?" He nodded in their direction.

"I've never walked on the dam. But I have been interested to see what all the hype is about," Daniel said. "Do you want to see the dam?" he asked Beth.

"Sure, why not? You only live once," Beth answered.

Ryan, Daniel, and Beth walked toward the house. I shook my head a bit until Amy pushed me, insinuating that she wanted to tag along.

"There's not much to see, just concrete and water," Claire added as the three of us caught up with the others.

We walked through the house, passed the cars in the front yard, crossed Lizardville Road, and stood on the embankment leading to the walkway. The ten-foot-wide walkway resembled a pier stretched out into a lake. But this was a creek. The water moved along at a fast pace. Ryan looked over his shoulder, gave me the nod of approval, and pointed for us to follow.

We descended the ten-foot embankment and set foot on the concrete slab. It resembled any ordinary sidewalk from back home. It didn't seem as dangerous as Mom and Dad had described. We pressed on until we reached the end, marked by a railing installed by the county.

"It doesn't look the same as Dad described," Daniel said, frowning.

"The dam once spanned nearly to the opposite bank of the creek. Its narrow opening caused the water to accumulate, generating a formidable current and undertow. The force was strong enough to drag someone under, risking their life potentially. Recognizing the danger, the county deemed it unsafe and sought to demolish the dam. However, the local fishing groups protested until they reached an agreement with the county. They removed half the dam, leaving what you see today. The larger gap allowed more water to pass and the river to flow naturally. Now it's gentler, and you can swim here. I should know because I have. It's also a great spot to go fishing. I know Dad, Parker, and I still fish here," Ryan said, smiling.

Amy pulled out her phone and snapped a few pictures for social media. We gathered together for a selfie while leaning over the metal railing. Daniel and Beth posed for a few individual pictures, some with the ladies and others with just the guys. We even had a few silly ones with the water in the background. Of course, Dad would be upset to learn we were on the dam, but I wasn't a kid anymore. I was twenty-four. None of us were kids. Beth was the youngest at twenty-one.

"This is pretty awesome. I wish I could have seen it as Dad described." I frowned. "I thought there was an old factory here?"

"When the county removed the dam, they also removed most of the factory remains, only leaving the concrete slabs you see over there," Ryan pointed. "Many are covered with weeds and grass. They are more visible in the winter months," Ryan added.

"What about Jimmy?" Daniel said, his tone sharp.

"Why do you ask?" Ryan tensed up.

"I was just curious," Daniel said. "Did they ever find his remains?" The sun faded as a cloud rolled over, sending a slight chill—a quick gust of wind whipped by. I watched as Daniel shivered. Beth and Amy did the same.

"We shouldn't be talking about…" Claire paused. "You know, Jimmy," she whispered.

"I think we should go back to the party," I mentioned, changing the subject.

"Aww, is Zack scared?" Ryan provoked.

"No, we came to spend time with family. That's all," I added.

"What do you think we are? We're all cousins." Ryan gave me a wry smile, spreading his hands out to cover all of us. "Well, except for Beth and Amy. I know a spot." Ryan smiled.

I could tell the others agreed and were intrigued by Ryan's comment. "Okay, but I don't want to be gone too long and worry Mom or Dad. "

"They'll be fine. Come on. Follow me." Ryan motioned, and we followed him to where the old factory once stood. "I didn't want to talk about Jimmy while standing on the dam. That's where he died." Ryan's voice rose, and then he paused for effect. "During all the construction, they never found his remains. Some thought the work would disturb his gravesite while others think he was washed downstream years ago. I think he still haunts this place today." Ryan's eyes glared at each of us.

I noticed a large crow perched on a nearby tree. I recalled Dad's stories about how big the crows were in Lizardville. I always thought it was a myth, yet he was right. The crow was double the typical size of any crow I had ever seen. I watched as the bird took flight. It circled above us a few times and cawed as it flew directly over our heads. We all ducked to avoid the attack. *Could that have been a warning?*

"Hey, I have an idea. Do you wanna see the cave?" Ryan motioned toward the woods.

"No, that's not a good idea. Besides, we don't have time." I was trying to make excuses, but to be fair, I was curious.

Daniel and Beth whispered among themselves. Amy nodded, and to my surprise, I was up for a walk. I looked at Ryan and nodded as did Daniel and Beth. We all stared at Claire. "I'm not going to say no if that's what you expect."

"I know where Parker keeps his camping gear. I'll grab a few things and meet you at the spring house. Claire, do you remember the way to the old spring house?" Ryan asked.

"Yeah, I can find it."

"Great. They won't see you if you go that way. I'll meet you at the spring house in ten minutes." Ryan smiled excitedly.

We followed Claire along Lizardville Road and away from Parker's house. We came to a small opening in the tree line. Claire crossed the road and entered, then motioned for us to follow. It was a good thing we had on jeans and sneakers. Amy wanted to wear a dress to impress my grandparents. Lucky for her, I talked her out of it. We pushed up a steep incline until we found a small house in the woods. It resembled a child's playhouse. There was no way an adult could even stand up inside.

"What is this?" Beth asked.

"It's a spring house. It covers the pump that supplies Uncle Parker's house with water. The small insulated house protects it from the environment," Claire said.

We gazed through the tree line. I noticed everyone at the party. It was apparent no one had noticed we were gone. The snapping of branches and the rustling of leaves startled us all. I looked around for something to grab to defend Amy and myself.

Ryan burst through the brush and scared us all with his scream. A small backpack was flung over his shoulders. "Follow me." He motioned as we pushed our way forward.

I pulled my phone from my pocket. It was almost 2:00. We had enough time to check out the cave and return before anyone would miss us. *Dad's going to be upset if he finds out.* "We need to be quick, alright?"

"No problem. It's not that far," Ryan said, and by the tone of his voice, I wasn't sure if I believed him.

We continued through the brushes until we merged with a small path. The walking became more manageable. No brush to push away. "How many people come up here?" I asked.

"This is a deer path. It's what's left of an old logging trail. They used to drag the logs down this path to the factory," Ryan said.

"No way. The loggers must have been powerful," Beth commented.

"No, silly, they strapped the logs behind a horse and pulled them out of the woods. This narrow walkway is all that's left of the road." Ryan smiled.

I was glad Beth asked the question because I wondered the same thing. We pushed forward, and the climb got steeper. We came to a small fork in the path and chose to stay to the right. We climbed up a small rock pile to a clearing in the trees. We paused, and Ryan pointed to the valley below. The view was amazing. We could see the outline of Fishing Creek, as well as a bit of the old dam and factory floor.

Everything was peaceful and quiet out here. Not like back in the city. "How far up do you think we are?" I asked.

"I would guess about two thousand feet. But don't hold me to it." Ryan chuckled.

"I forgot to mention that we should be on the lookout for poison ivy. They are reddish at this time of year and are in leaves of three." Ryan smiled. "There's an old saying: 'Leaves of three, let them be.'" Ryan pointed to a cluster of poison ivy a few yards away. "You don't want to spend the rest of your vacation with a horrible rash. The itching will drive you nuts."

We looked at each other and nodded. Ryan was more of a survivalist than any of us who grew up in the city.

"I'm thirsty. Do you have any water?" Amy asked. She looked tired, too. I know I was feeling a bit exhausted. I wasn't used to walking this far, let alone uphill.

"No water, but we are only about ten minutes from the pond and cave entrance. Let's get moving," Ryan insisted.

We pushed through the dense foliage, the branches snapping and leaves crunching beneath our feet. For ten minutes, we shuffled forward, our pace steady but our senses heightened by the rustling wilderness around us. Suddenly, Ryan's voice cut through the ambient sounds. "Do you hear that?" he whispered.

We stopped talking and listened. I could hear the water crashing into a pool. "Is that the waterfall? We found it," I said excitedly.

Ryan pulled out a large knife.

"What's that for?" I asked.

"You can never be too prepared."

Ryan turned, pushed some branches to one side, and cut a few off with the knife. *Dang, that is one sharp knife.* Ryan pulled a large branch back, allowing us to pass. I followed the gang until we stepped into the clearing.

It was just like Dad described. Over a rock-face wall, a small waterfall cascaded about twelve or fifteen feet into a small crystal-clear pond. This place was amazing. I pulled out my phone and snapped a few pictures. I noticed it was after 3:00. I tried to text Dad, but there was no service.

SIX

My mouth hung open. This was prettier than Mom or Dad had ever described. Everyone was in awe of the picturesque scene. Amy couldn't stop gushing over how pretty the falls were.

"Looks can be deceiving, guys," Ryan said, snapping us out of the moment. "Be on the lookout for anything out of the norm. If you're thirsty, now's the time. Use your hand to scoop up some water and drink up."

I dipped my hand in the water and quickly snapped it back. Ryan laughed and added that the water was about fifty-five degrees. "But you won't taste anything better."

I scooped my hand under and pulled it toward my mouth. *Dang, this was excellent-tasting water.* Amy, Beth, and Claire all did the same. "Are you alright?" I asked.

"Yes, this place is amazing," Daniel responded.

I noticed Ryan had finished drinking his water and made his way to the rock wall. He pulled on a bunch of branches, moving them away from the surface, revealing an opening. *There is a cave!* I swallowed my last bit of water and walked over to help Ryan. He stood tall and motioned us over. I glanced back at the others still drinking. I poked my head inside. The room was dark and open, and I could tell we had hit paydirt. I couldn't wait to get inside and explore.

"Hey, look what Ryan found." I motioned for the others to see. Daniel stepped forward out of curiosity. Claire stood and dashed to our side to get a better look.

"I'm in," Claire said eagerly. "Why didn't you show me this before?" She slugged Ryan in the arm.

Daniel stuck his head inside, pulled out, put his left leg inside, followed by his right leg, and disappeared into the wall. Ryan handed me a flashlight. I turned it on and went in after my brother. We looked from side to side and top to bottom. This was bigger than we could have imagined. Amy entered next, followed by Beth, Claire, and Ryan. We had three flashlights, and he also had some rope in his backpack.

"Where to?" I asked, like a kid who spotted a dozen presents under the Christmas tree. My heart thumped hard. I squeezed Amy's hand. I didn't expect her to understand like Daniel or myself. We grew up hearing Dad's stories, and here we were, living and exploring inside the cave he talked about.

"Follow me." Ryan motioned for us to follow. "Stay close together. Make sure you can always touch the person next to you," Ryan said. I trusted him and could tell he felt responsible for our lives.

We marched forward some fifteen or twenty yards. The cave had a musty smell. It tickled my nose. I could tell we were descending at a gradual rate. We paused when the girls wanted to take a few selfies so they could share them on social media. *City girls have gone country*! I chuckled at my thought.

"What's so funny?" Amy asked.

"Nothing."

"Oh, come on, please share," she begged, nudging my shoulder.

"It's nice seeing you having a great time. I thought you might get bored being away from the city," I replied.

"It's exciting seeing where your mom and dad grew up. This brings the story Parker told last night to a new level," Amy said.

"I agree with that." I gave her a little kiss.

Ryan motioned us to move on. He said he wanted to find the room where they claimed the body was buried. We jumped and turned toward the entrance, or what was now our only exit, when we heard a commotion. Squawking caws from a crow echoed throughout the chamber. I couldn't tell if it was one crow or several. The echoes lasted for several minutes, and we covered our ears and pushed deeper into the cave as we tried to escape the noise.

"I didn't think crows flew inside caves, only bats," I said.

"I would guess it found its way inside when we left the entrance open. I'm sure he's trying to find his way out, and that is what we hear," Ryan said.

Everything Ryan said made sense. He signaled for us to stop. "Turn out your light." We did, and so did Ryan. The place went pitch black. "Put your hand in front of your face," Ryan instructed us. I moved my hand in front of my face and couldn't see anything.

"That's cool," I said, and everyone agreed. Ryan turned his light on, and I noticed Amy and Beth still waving their hands. I smiled. We continued forward. I watched where I placed my feet while trying to enjoy everything around me.

Ryan suddenly stopped. I stepped forward and noticed a steep incline. It appeared wet, just like Mom and Dad had claimed in their story. Here we were, ready to slide down as my parents did when they were kids. This was exciting. A shiver raced down my spine, and goosebumps broke out on my forearms.

"Who wants to go first?" Ryan asked.

"I'll go." I inched forward and shined my light downward. It wasn't that far, but it was steep. Ryan braced his foot against a large rock and tossed the rope. He wrapped one end around himself while I took the other and used it to control my slide. I quickly lost my footing and ended up on my rear until I reached the bottom.

"Are you alright?" Ryan asked.

"I'm fine. Just a little wet." I chuckled. Amy was next, and I kept tension on the line so she had something to hold on to. But she, like myself, ended up sliding on her butt. Beth, then Daniel, followed by Claire, and finally Ryan, who slid down like a surfer on the ocean.

"What about the rope?" I questioned.

"I wrapped it around the boulder, so we can use it to pull ourselves up," Ryan said.

"Good thinking," Daniel said, and I agreed.

We pushed forward and deeper into the cavern. Ryan told us to focus on the left side. Five or ten minutes passed, and there was an opening on the left-hand side. Ryan shined the light up in his face. "I think we found what we were looking for," Ryan said.

One by one, we all took a peek inside the small room on the left. I couldn't help but notice the old fold-up shovel leaning against the wall. They used them for camping. Mom and Dad had told us about this. So far, everything they said checked out. *Oh, my goodness. Can all of this be real? Everything they said was correct. Can there be ghosts?* I wasn't sold yet. But everything was adding up.

Ryan explained that the shovel was a prop Uncle Buck had planted here to help sell the story. Well, they had me convinced. But one thing puzzled me. *Mom and Dad never discussed this with any of their friends. Only us boys, and he didn't want Parker telling us the stories last night, either. Now, I was puzzled. Why stage things and never talk about them? Something freaked Mom and Dad out when they were kids. That's why we didn't come back to Lizardville often.*

"We better head back," Ryan said as he glanced at his phone. I pulled mine from my pocket and snapped pictures of the room and the shovel. I looked at the time and knew everyone at the party knew we had left by now. We couldn't be gone for hours without being noticed.

We walked toward the opening. We halted at the foot of the slippery incline. Ryan took the lead, followed by Daniel, who was tasked with assisting the girls. I remained at the rear, ensuring everyone ascended safely. The process took some time, but eventually the girls reached the top. Ryan then retrieved the rope and encouraged me to make a dash for the summit. *Why not? I'm sure I can do this, and that would impress Amy.* I took a few steps back and then burst forward. I made it halfway before I lost my footing and slid back to the bottom. My second attempt was better than the first. But I still produced the same results.

Ryan finally tossed me the rope and helped me. I was thankful I tried but slightly embarrassed that I could not do it. We continued until we noticed a light in the distance. Our exit was in sight. We only had one problem. A large white bear was sitting in front of the opening.

Ryan motioned for us to stop and raised his finger to his lips to silence us. Amy wrapped her arm around mine, and I noticed her lips quivering. Beth stood behind Daniel, and Claire slowly moved behind Ryan.

"What are we going to do?" I whispered to Ryan.

"I don't know," Ryan said, his voice shaky.

"Have you ever seen a bear before? Can we scare him away?" I questioned.

"I had one run-in with a brown bear, but Dad was with me, and he held his hands out to his sides and yelled, and it ran away." Ryan appeared nervous. That did not make me or the others feel comfortable. "But I've never seen a white bear before." He gave me a side-eye look.

"Let's back up a little, so the bear doesn't notice us," Ryan suggested.

We slowly moved backward, making as little noise as possible. Ryan turned off his light, and I did the same. Ryan turned his back on and suggested we need one light to see. We moved to the right behind a few larger rocks. "We wait here."

"How long?" I whispered, my heart pounding against my ribs. "What if the bear decides to come closer?" My voice trembled, betraying the panic rising within me. The bear rose onto its hind legs, towering over us with a menacing presence as if in response. I could feel the adrenaline surging through my veins, a primal instinct urging me to flee. But the bear returned to all fours and began to advance toward us. I knew escape wasn't an option.

JOHN

SEVEN

Parker and Buck emerged from the house, carrying two backpacks. "Good news: one of my packs is gone, so they must be heading to the cave," Parker said.

"I'm not sure that's good news. What if something happens?" Sara's voice trembled.

"It's going to be alright. We'll find them, I promise," I said, looking at Buck for reassurance.

"We'll find them." Buck nodded. "We shouldn't be gone long," Buck added.

"You think you're going without us?" Lexi snapped. "Not a chance. My daughter's out there, and nobody knows what they might be up against."

"I agree," Sara said as she walked toward the path. "Are we going or not?" She turned and yelled at the rest of us.

I snapped out of my daze. I told Mom and Dad we would be back shortly. Buck, Parker, and I jogged to catch up with the ladies who were walking at a brisk pace. I was not looking forward to the hike, let alone what we might find. Every time we went to the cave, we had unexpected visitors. Anabelle tried to stop us the first time. Annabelle, Jimmy, and Donald Thornhill another time. I didn't want another ghost encounter. I'd seen enough ghosts for one lifetime.

We continued our fast pace. *Are Sara and Lexi trying to give me a heart attack? I guess I have to get a gym membership or start doing some exercises the minute we get home.* Sara always told me to work out more. I reminded her that she didn't, yet she claimed she did enough running at the hospital as a nurse. I guess she was right. Sara always had a way of inspiring me. She and Lexi were walking like two ladies on a mission.

As we ventured farther, the familiarity of our surroundings grew. Though my visits to this place had been infrequent during childhood, the memories flooded back with surprising clarity. Perhaps the countless retellings of our shared stories etched them deeply in my mind. I retrieved my phone and checked for any missed calls or messages, but there were none. Only then did I realize I had no service—a revelation that sparked a glimmer of hope that perhaps the boys were facing the same predicament.

I planned on taking a few pictures when we got there. That way, I'd have proof to back up my stories. We came to the fork in the path. I knew we were getting close. "Can we take a break?" I asked.

"We're almost there. Let's keep going!" Sara yelled.

I frowned but pushed forward. I could use a drink of water. Sara had one thing on her mind: our boys. She always protected them more than I preferred. But I wasn't going to stand in her way. Sara stopped and placed a hand on her ear. We stopped, and I could hear the water hitting the pond. *Thank goodness!* I could get a drink shortly.

"Turn around," a male voice whispered in my ear. I was startled initially and glanced at Sara, Lexi, and the others. *"Turn around,"* the voice said again. I had to be the only one hearing this. I ignored the voice and pushed forward with the others.

We moved forward and then came to a spot in the path where the brush was parted. That was a great sign. That meant someone recently went this way. We followed the same route until the pond and waterfall came into view. It was prettier than I remembered. I pulled out my phone and snapped a few pictures.

"No!" Sara screamed.

I glanced in her direction and then to the wall where my eyes were fixed. The bushes covered the rock wall. If the kids had found the cave, they would have had to move the brush out of the way. *Where can they be? Did they try to find this place and get lost?* My heart sank into my chest. I sat on one of the logs at the water's edge. I needed to stay calm. I didn't want Sara freaking out.

"What the heck?" Lexi paced back and forth and tugged at her hair. "They must be lost in the woods!" she shouted.

That was the last thing Sara or I wanted to hear. I wrapped my arm around her. "We'll find them, I promise."

"That doesn't make sense. Ryan knows where this place is. I brought him here a time or two. We even went into the cave," Buck mumbled to himself.

"Maybe they went past the dam, then walked the path along Fishing Creek?" Parker said.

Parker's observation struck a chord: had our journey been in vain? Were the children at the party growing concerned about our absence? The absence of technology left me feeling utterly helpless. "Does anyone have cell service?" I glanced at my phone again, hoping for a signal. Despite the shaking of heads around me, no one seemed to share my concern. It suddenly struck me: *They don't have a cell tower out here? Why put them in the mountains? It would certainly help hunters, but this is Lizardville—home to a thousand people.*

"So, what now?" I asked, scooping a handful of water and raising it to my lips. Parker pulled a canteen from his pack. He gulped some water and then dipped it in the pond to fill it up.

"You had water all this time?" I asked.

"Yes," Parker paused, "I don't remember anyone asking for a drink. I have a few energy bars, too, in case you're hungry."

My mouth hung open. Buck took one of the energy bars, peeling back the wrapper and taking a bite as he sat on the other end of the log. "So, we head back down the mountain, check the party, and then walk along the path next to the creek?" Buck asked.

"One problem with that: there's cell service along the creek." Parker stared at each of us. "I know because I've called home a few times, even called you once." Parker pointed at Lexi.

"I remember." Lexi smiled. "You asked me if I wanted the fish you caught or if you should toss them back in the creek," Lexi replied.

"Dang, sis, you remembered that?" Parker smiled.

"You're right, but now we don't have cell service, so where does that leave us?" I asked, keeping my mind in the task at hand. "Where are the kids?"

"Maybe they pulled the branches over the entrance after they went inside." Lexi sounded optimistic.

I nodded and watched Parker walk toward the wall. He paused and pulled back the branches. He was revealing the entrance to a place I hated. This place brought back haunting memories. That was why I didn't want to bring my family here. Parker disappeared inside. Buck handed Parker one of the backpacks. Sara, Lexi, and I stood in line waiting to enter. I glanced upward and back to the tree line. That was a good sign, but there were no large birds.

"*Turn around*," the male voice whispered. I closed my eyes. I knew the voice was only in my head. I took a deep breath and helped Sara inside, telling her to be careful. I then lent a hand to Lexi. I paused. I inhaled, my heart racing, swallowed hard, and put one foot inside, then the other. "*You're making a mistake*," the voice insisted. Once again, I ignored his warning. I adjusted to the dark until a flashlight blinded me. Buck and Parker chuckled.

"Would you grow up?" I snapped. "The kids are missing. That should be our focus." I shook my head. Sara placed her hand on my arm for comfort.

"Lighten up, man. My son is missing too," Buck added.

Buck was right. I gave him a little push and smiled. I looked around the cavern. The place was just like I remembered it. I pulled out my phone and snapped a few pictures. Now, when I told the stories, I'd have visuals. "What next? Do we go deeper?" I asked.

"Zack! Daniel!" Sara yelled, cupping her hands around her mouth. Her voice echoed off the walls.

"Or we could do that." Lexi giggled, pointing to her sister.

Something farther down the slope caught my attention. I pointed into the cavern, and Buck turned his light in that direction. Something moved. I wasn't sure what, but Buck and I started walking forward. Sara yelled again. The object moved again, this time standing up. Buck and I froze. Sara, Lexi, and Parker were only two steps behind.

Parker added more light so we could get a better look. My worst fear was coming true—a bear. The bear stood on his hind feet. He was taller than any bear I had ever seen. I took a step back and bumped into Sara. The bear was solid white. Could he be an albino? I'd never seen a white bear before. I was puzzled and intrigued, to say the least. I've seen weird, unexplained things in my life, but this was a first.

"What do we do?" Lexi whispered.

Parker extended his hands over his head, appearing taller than he was. Buck raised his hands over his head. If the bear felt threatened, he would back down and go deeper into the cave, allowing us a chance to escape. But the only reason we came in here in the first place was to find the kids, and this bear was blocking the path.

I stepped forward, grabbed the light from Buck, and began to walk toward the bear. Something was off. The bear didn't seem to be threatened. He didn't move much, and he sat back down. What fascinated me was the light seemed to pass through the bear. I continued to walk toward the bear. The others were only a few steps behind. The bear stood once again as if he was telling me to stop. I didn't heed the warning. I stopped about twenty yards away. This was not a real bear. He was fading.

"Jimmy?" I called out. The bear sat down, staring at me, almost pleading with me for help. "Jimmy, is that you? It's me, Johnny. That's Sara, Lexi, Buck, and Parker." I pointed to each one as I called their name. The bear growled when I mentioned Parker. "It is you!" Overwhelmed with relief, I hugged him. The temperature suddenly plunged. The bear stood and growled. "Jimmy, it's me. It's Johnny, your best friend," I begged him to remember.

"Mom? Dad?" Zack's voice echoed in the cavern. I looked past the bear and saw a group of people huddled about fifty yards away near the wall. "The bear!" Zack yelled.

I shook my head like I couldn't see the bear standing before me. Sometimes, my boys said the darndest things.

"Jimmy, show yourself. The real you," I begged. "Please, I missed you."

"Is that why you never came back? You missed me?" I recognized Jimmy's voice. It hadn't changed, and why would it? He was still a thirteen-year-old boy, or should I say ghost?

"It's not like that."

"Oh, tell me what it's like," Jimmy barked.

Zack, Daniel, and the others slowly walked toward us. They looked fine, not hurt, maybe a bit shaken from the bear trapping them in the cave. I could see the surprised look on Zack's face, perhaps disbelief that I was talking to a bear, or it could be that the bear had not eaten us yet.

Jimmy, the bear, turned and roared at the kids. They pressed themselves tight against the wall. The girls were horrified. Ryan used himself as a shield to protect the others.

I took another step closer. "Jimmy, please show yourself," I begged again. "I want to see you." I extended my hands to him. "Please." I frowned.

Jimmy's demeanor softened, and as if by magic, the bear diminished in size while a swirling white mist enveloped it in a circular motion. The bear vanished instantly, leaving only a tall, slim figure wearing corduroy shorts with no shirt. The translucent form of the figure hovered about a foot above the ground.

Zack and Daniel watched in amazement. Beth sank to the ground, and Amy joined her. I remember how I felt the first time I saw a ghost. It was something that would stick with you for life. If you told people, no one believed you.

I frowned, then looked at Jimmy. "You look the same," I said in disbelief.

"Of course, I look the same. I will always look like this!" I could tell Jimmy was angry. "One day, when you die, you will understand!" Jimmy roared. "Let me show you what I can do." He whirled his hands above his head. The wind began to whip in a circle, forming a small tornado. We watched it grow until it filled the room.

"Stop it," I said. I bowed my head and covered my face. "Jimmy, stop it now!" I hollered. I caught a glimpse of Zack, Daniel, and the others crouched down on the ground. This had to stop immediately. "What did I ever do to hurt you?" I asked. I couldn't understand why he hated me so much. He must have learned some of these tricks from Annabelle or possibly Donald Thornhill.

"Are you afraid of a little wind?" The wind ceased, and Jimmy glared at me with gritted teeth.

"Help me understand why you are upset?" I asked.

"You, Buck, and Parker abandoned me. You left me here to live in solitude. Do you have any idea what that will do to a person?" Jimmy yelled. He gritted his teeth and growled. Jimmy reminded me of a wild animal. *Maybe that's why he took the shape of a bear.*

"I'm sorry. We never meant to hurt you or anyone. Life continued for us. We grew up, got married, had children. We have jobs; we're adults now, so try to understand." I pleaded my case the best I could, but from the look on his face, Jimmy wasn't buying what I was selling. I didn't know what else to say.

"Jimmy, we missed you and thought of you all the time," Lexi said.

"Aww? Is that why you never come to the woods? Or call my name?" He threw his arms out in disgust. "Is that why my best friend never came to see me?" Jimmy pointed at me. "Go ahead, try and explain that!" Jimmy yelled.

Sara and Lexi both shot me an evil look. I sank. I was feeling guilty for not coming home. *I was only trying to protect myself and my children from the memories. I don't know why that is so hard for everyone to believe.* "I was scared to come home. The last time I spoke with ghosts, it wasn't pleasant." A tear traced down my cheek.

"I'm not falling for your fake tears. How would you like it if I took one of the kids and made them my friend?" Jimmy threatened, giving me an evil eye. "Or what if I took your son?" He pointed at Buck. "How about I take your daughter? She's pretty." Jimmy chuckled, sending Lexi into a tizzy. Buck balled his fist and was ready to lunge at Jimmy. Lexi stood in disbelief. Jimmy, once our friend, was now threatening our children.

"A word of advice: watch your back!" Jimmy vanished.

EIGHT

Amy and Beth stood and dashed to Sara, who embraced them. Zack and Daniel ran to me and wrapped their arms around me. I couldn't hug them enough. Lexi held Claire as Buck and Ryan embraced. Parker patted Ryan's back as I watched, looking over my boy's shoulders.

"Dad, I can't believe this. It's impossible," Zack burst as he pushed me away. "How could you put our lives in danger?" Zack asked.

"What?" I was stunned by the accusation.

"I can't even begin to tell you. Oh crap, I don't even know what to say. I'm just mad!" Daniel exclaimed, waving his hands like he was trying to get a bee away from his face.

"I understand your frustration. I do. But I don't think you should blame me for this. I've been telling you these stories for years." I tried to calm them down. I glanced at Sara; the girls were still crying in her arms. *Gosh, just a few hours ago, they were all happy. Now, they are frightened little children.*

"Dad, you're a writer. You tell fiction all the time. I thought this was just one of your cockamamie stories. How in the world is this true? Was that real?" Zack trembled. He was taking this worse than I did the first time I saw a ghost.

"That wasn't real." Daniel pushed away and walked in circles, repeating the same thing. "That wasn't real."

"Relax. Take a deep breath." I paused. I took a deep breath to show them how by moving my hands up and down. I breathed in and then out.

"Listen up!" Lexi yelled. She stood next to Claire. "Everyone out of the cave." Buck, Parker, and Ryan moved toward the opening. "Move it!" she hollered. Nudging Sara and the girls along, I did the same with the boys. One by one, we left the cave. Lexi and I were the last two out. I pushed my way through the opening. I squinted and moved my left hand to cover my vision from the sun. I had forgotten it was summer and still daylight.

Lexi ushered everyone forward and motioned for them to sit on the log. "Now that everyone is outside and seated, let me tell you a few things. The stories you all heard as kids were not lies or make-believe. They were real." She paused to let that sink in. "Yes, you saw a ghost today. You met Jimmy. He's our friend," Lexi said. "Or was," she recanted.

"Some friend. He tried to kill us," Beth whimpered.

"All of you have so much to learn about the spirit world. They do a lot of talking and little harm. Yes, they can move things, like the wind, make it cold, but it's mostly talk," Lexi said.

"What about possessing your body? Well? What about that?" Daniel snapped. I startled Daniel when I laid my hand on his shoulder.

"Sorry, I didn't mean to scare you."

"You didn't mean to scare me? Then why in the heck did you bring me here?" Daniel shouted. I looked to Sara for advice. She still had her arm around Beth and Amy.

"Please calm down. This isn't helping anyone." I motioned to each of them. "We're all adults. What you saw in the cave was a ghost, a spirit." I took a deep breath. This entire experience had my nerves on edge, and my fingers twitched. At first, my boys and their girlfriends were upset with me because Jimmy threatened everyone. *Who says things are not going well?* "This is part of the reason why I didn't want to stay the week." I gazed at everyone, and the waterfall splashing into the pond gave a calming tone. "Ghosts are real. You can choose not to believe what happened in the cave, but it did. The stories I have told you since you were thirteen years old were real, not some phony made-up story so I could scare you. No, they were real. We all went through a lot when we were kids. Maybe now you will understand why I act a little strange sometimes, or your mother jumps at the slightest thing. This is why," I said, pointing toward the cave.

"So, now what?" Zack asked in a calm voice. "I mean, he threatened us, all of us."

"Yes, he threatened us. This is not the first time a ghost has threatened us," I said casually. "We need to return to the party and enjoy the rest of the day. Say nothing to no one." Zack and Daniel glared at me. "Do you want to put the rest of the family in danger?" My voice intended to put a little fear in the boys. "Then we'll need to devise a plan," I said.

"We could contact Old Man Smithers," Lexi said.

"What? He passed away," I added.

"Yes, but that doesn't mean he can't help us. I think he likes me living in his house," Lexi said.

"Mom, you mean we live with a ghost?" Claire said, slightly panicked.

"Ah, yeah, kind of," Lexi replied.

"Oh my gosh, now you tell me. I took a shower there. He saw me naked," Claire gushed.

"Oh, my goodness, he's harmless." Lexi smiled.

"You're telling me Old Man Smithers is a ghost?" I asked excitedly.

"I've never seen him, but I sometimes feel his presence. He also whispers things. I'm not sure what he said. I know he would help us. We need to have a séance to bring him out."

"Are you nuts?" Amy blurted. "We don't need to do anything. I need to go home tonight!" she added. Zack held her tight for comfort. She closed her eyes and swayed in his arms.

"What makes you think the spirits won't follow you home?" Ryan mentioned. "No, we have to finish this once and for all," Ryan said.

"I hate to agree with you, Ryan, but you make a valid point. We need to finish this. Dad, how do we close the spirit world? Or send Jimmy to the other side?" Daniel said excitedly.

"It's not that easy. First, we need to find out what's keeping Jimmy here. Then solve the problem," Buck said.

"I remember the last time I spoke with you. The day after the cemetery battle, he said he wouldn't tell me where his remains are. If we find them and bury him, he could finally rest," I said.

"There's only one problem with your plan. For over thirty years, his remains have been missing. You think we are just going to magically find them?" Parker said.

"What other options do we have?" I looked around to see if anyone else had any suggestions.

"Maybe Old Man Smithers can find out where they are. This would save us time. We find out where they are, grab them, take them to the cemetery, and this all ends. Just like you guys did years ago," Daniel said, gazing at us.

"It worked once, but I doubt it will work again. Old Man Smithers, Tom Evans, and Gladys were key to our success. Without them, I'm not sure we can pull this off." I frowned, knowing what we had to accomplish. *But how?*

"Tom Evans lives at the Salona nursing home," Parker said.

I leaned back, and my mouth dropped. "Are you kidding? Gosh, I would love to see him while I'm in town," I said with an ear-to-ear smile. I had written him several letters, and then we exchanged emails. But one day, they all stopped. I only assumed he passed away like his mother, Gladys, and Bob Smithers. We all have an expiration date; time has a way of doing that.

"I have a plan," I announced. Now that we were calm, I had everyone's attention. "Sara and I should swing by the nursing home and see if we can visit Tom. Let me find out what his thoughts are about Jimmy. Any questions?"

"Then what?" Lexi asked.

"One thing at a time. I was thinking we visit Tom. Then try to reach Bob Smithers, so you must brush up on your séance powers. Let's see what we learn, and if it's possible to locate Jimmy's remains and get him to cross over. Maybe one of them will have another idea." I sounded chipper and optimistic. "Any thoughts or concerns? Questions?" A few light nods and some scrunched-up noses. *I'm going to take that as a yes.*

Jimmy's remains had to be what was keeping him here. *Yes, it could be something else, but what?* "We tell no one of today's events and work as a team to solve the problem. Is everyone okay with this?" I waited for all to agree. I was nervous about Amy and Beth. They were the only outsiders. The rest of us were family and had a more significant stake in this game. I flashed a giant smile and rose to my feet, patting the boys on the back, and watched as Sara gave Amy and Beth one more hug.

I took Sara's arm, and we started down the mountain. I heard Zack whisper to Amy that she needed to trust me. I believe I listened to a yes—one more on board. Now, I needed to convince Beth that this was the right thing to do.

Soon, I could see the back of Parker's house through the tree line. As we approached, I could hear laughter and people talking. We cleared the tree line. My mom greeted us. "I was beginning to wonder where you went," Mom said.

"Showing the kids around the woods a bit, that's all." I hugged her.

"The apple pie is great. You better get a slice before it's gone," Dad said as he shoved pie into his mouth.

Pie sounded good. "Anyone else want a piece?" I asked.

"No thanks. How can you eat pie right now?" Sara softly said.

"I worked up an appetite after that walk." I smiled and went to the dessert table. Dad was right. The pie tasted terrific. One by one, the party broke up, and later that evening, we made our way back to Lexi's house.

I wondered if Tom would offer any suggestions. *What about Bob Smithers?* I stared at the ceiling, listening to Sara breathe. *How can she lay her head down and doze off so quickly?* Wondering about this was not going to help me sleep. I tried counting and thinking of nothing. I decided to keep my eyes closed and listen to the silence.

NINE

I rolled to my side. Sara was gone. I knew I was awake. I could see the sun beaming through a crack in the curtains. I never heard Sara get out of bed. That was not like me. I tilted my head toward the door. I heard female voices. I recognized Sara's and then Lexi's. I pulled the blanket back, swung my legs over the side, and planted my feet on the floor.

My slippers were next to the bed. I wasn't sure if I had put them there or Sara had. I guess it didn't matter. I slipped them on and walked to the door. I stepped into the hallway to the beautiful smell of bacon. My mouth began to water. *Bacon!* That was my weakness.

"Look who finally woke up?" Sara laughed.

"I thought you were an early riser," Lexi added.

"10:15!" I shouted. "Oh my gosh, how could I sleep this late?" I needed to shower, eat, and go to the nursing home.

"John, relax. We have all day. Tom's not going anywhere." Sara smiled.

"Um, guess not," I said. I breathed in, then exhaled. Sara was right. She had this way of reading me and knowing what I was thinking. It was scary if I thought about it. I was never going to keep any secrets from her.

"Take a seat." Lexi poured me a cup of coffee.

It tasted great, just what I needed. "Are the kids awake?" I asked.

"Not yet," Sara responded.

"Did you check on them?" I replied quickly.

"Chill out, John," Sara snapped. "You have been acting weird ever since we arrived. What is going on with you?"

"I've been hearing voices. Male voices. I heard them again yesterday while hiking up the mountain. Warnings!" I opened up to Sara and Lexi. I trusted them. The last thing we needed was to panic the kids. *It's funny how I still call them kids when they are all in their twenties. They will always be my kids.*

"Drink your coffee, have a slice of toast, and relax," Sara instructed.

Lexi placed a jar of apple butter before me. I hadn't had any in years. It looked divine. I snatched the jar, twisted the lid, and layered it on my toast. Now, who was acting like a child? I savored the moment. The apple butter melted in my mouth. I was in heaven.

"Julie, Farmer Frank's wife, made it from scratch. It's awesome," Lexi said.

I nodded my head while taking another mouthwatering bite. I finished my coffee and returned for a second piece of toast and apple butter. I felt relaxed now. The door flew open, and Zack and Amy came bursting inside.

"Everything alright?" I said, startled at first.

"Yes, Amy won. We raced. What's for breakfast?" Zack said.

"Sausage, bacon, eggs, and toast. If you want something else, I also have cereal." Lexi pointed toward the cabinets.

"That all sounds amazing. Thank you, Mrs. Parker," Amy said.

"Mrs. Parker is my mother. Please call me Lexi," she said—a hint of anger in her voice.

I moved to the sofa to allow room at the table. I enjoyed watching Zack and Amy fix themselves a plate. It felt like only yesterday when I told Zack and Daniel the story of my childhood, and here they were today, young men fending for themselves.

Sara nudged me as she sat next to me. "What time did you want to leave?" she whispered.

"I'm not sure. Who's all going?"

"Um, I guess you and me." Sara grinned. "Unless you want Lexi to tag along."

"Sure, the three of us should go. We don't want too many of us, or that will raise suspicion," I said. "Let me get ready, and we can leave."

Sara smiled and made her way to Lexi. I watched Sara whisper something in Lexi's ear as I headed down the hallway. I went into the bathroom. I turned on the shower.

"*I warned you*," a husky voice echoed in my ear.

I spun to find an empty room. *Why does this keep happening to me? Am I the only one who hears voices? Maybe because I have the closest connection to everything. I don't know. I guess I will never know.* I hopped in the shower and cleaned up. *Thank goodness I don't hear any voices in here. The last thing I want is to take a shower with a ghost.*

I chuckled to myself. I toweled off, danced across the hall, changed clothes, and was ready to go.

Twenty minutes later, I returned to the family room. I was stunned to find Lexi and Sara ready to go. For once, they were waiting on me. We said our goodbyes and walked to the car. I was happy when Lexi volunteered to drive. They sat up front and chatted the entire way to the nursing home.

We used to stop by the general store when Tom owned it. I'm guessing the last time was ten or twelve years ago. I wondered if he would remember me. Tom had played an essential part in my childhood. I know he shared many things with me, but deep inside, I knew he had secrets he didn't share, such as his connection with Old Man Smithers.

The car rolled to a stop. I suddenly felt my stomach twist. Lexi and Sara got out, and I followed. I glanced around. I don't know why I thought we would find trouble here. I didn't see anything out of the ordinary or large birds. I looked at the building. *Wow, this place is lovely*. It must have been new. I would have remembered this building. I followed the ladies up the sidewalk, then darted ahead to open the door for them. The main lobby was small, and the receptionist sat behind a glass window.

"Hello, may I help you?" the young lady said.

"Yes, we are here to see Tom Evans." Sara smiled.

"Do you have an appointment?" We were a little stunned. I didn't know you needed an appointment to visit a friend or relative in a nursing home.

"No, ma'am, we don't," Sara said.

"Are you a relative?"

"No, just close friends," Sara replied.

"Hi, I'm John Malone. I worked for many years at the general store with Tom. I'm in town visiting relatives and wanted to say hello," I said after I stepped forward.

"Oh, I remember that place. My mom loved how Tom took care of her car."

"Tom was a great guy," I added. She handed us a few clipboards and requested that we fill them out. Once complete, we laid them on the counter, and she verified our driver's licenses and paperwork individually.

She asked us to take a seat and then made a phone call. She said they would set up a guest room so we could have some privacy. I thought that was nice.

I pulled out my phone, but they called our names before I could check my email. We entered a grand hall where many residents sat watching a large-screen television. Others played board games or card games. We continued down a hallway, and she stopped and pointed to our left.

I turned the corner, and Tom sat in an oversized chair. He smiled the minute I entered, and then he stood, sagging in pain. His face was etched in sorrow, and his skin color slightly faded. He wrapped his arms around me and pulled me tight. "It's great to see you, Johnny," he rasped.

"You look amazing, Tom. Do you remember Sara and Lexi?" I pointed to them. "Sara and I are married." I smiled.

"I may be old, son, but you told me that the last time you were in town." Tom snorted. He walked to Sara, hugged her, and then Lexi. "Are you still single, Lexi?" Tom whispered. Lexi chuckled. "Yes."

"Don't blame me for asking. You are the prettiest thing I've seen in a long time," Tom said, lifting an eyebrow.

"I see you haven't lost your sense of humor," I said.

"So, what brings you back to Lizardville?" Tom cut right to the chase as he sat back in his chair.

"We came in town for a family reunion. I thought I would stop to see you while we were here," I said.

"You didn't invite me to the reunion?" Tom huffed. Then he gave us a wry smile.

"I didn't think about it. I'm sorry," Lexi whimpered and grimaced.

"It's alright. I understand. Who needs an old fellow like me hanging around?" Tom said.

My heart sank. "Tom, I'm sorry. We would have picked you up and brought you to the house if I had known. After all, you are my family. That's why I only visit every ten years." I chuckled.

"Yeah, yeah, yeah," Tom scoffed. "Anyway, now that we have the pleasantries out of the way, did you come to get me out of here?"

"I didn't know you were allowed to leave," Lexi said. I nodded in agreement.

"Yes, we're allowed time away with family members, and you are the closest thing I have to family. That's why they let you in, Johnny. I had your name on the list as family," Tom said.

That touched my heart. "Can you leave today?" I asked.

"No, but we can fill out the request form to get me out of here tomorrow." Tom smiled. "I would love to see the store and ride around for a bit before returning to your place," Tom added.

"Did you know Lexi bought Bob Smithers' house after he passed away?" I asked.

Tom's eyes grew wide, and his mouth hung open. "I didn't know that. Can we go to your house, Lexi?"

"Of course," Lexi said. "I'm sure that will bring back some old memories."

Tom pushed a little buzzer on the table. A moment later, one of the staff entered. Tom requested a leave form, and they nodded and left, only to return moments later.

The nurse handed me the paperwork and told me to fill it out so she could process the request. Typically, they requested three days' notice, but they were making an exception for me since I was in town for only a short time.

Tom's smile grew wider. I could see the excitement on his face. We finished our visit and left an hour later. I couldn't wait to get Tom out of there and back to Lexi's to discuss what happened in the cave and the voices I'd heard.

After leaving the nursing home, I called the boys, and we met over at my parents' house. We chatted about our memories as kids. Zack and Daniel's grandpa told them more stories. I didn't remember some of them; who knew if they were true? The entire time, my mind was elsewhere. Could Tom help convince Bob Smithers to help us? I guess I would find out tomorrow.

TEN

Birds were chirping and playing on the window sill. The sun was rising, and Mother Nature was waking up. One by one, we prepped for the day. Amy and Beth wanted to try their hand at fishing. Zack and Daniel might not be the best teachers, so I called Buck and Parker. They agreed to swing by and help. Claire seemed to have quite a bit of knowledge about the subject and didn't want her uncle ruining things, but it was too late. I already made the call. They all promised to stay out of the woods. I didn't expect us to be gone long. I trusted the boys to behave. Yet they promised the other day and ended up in the cave.

Lexi said she would drive. We strode toward the car, and just like yesterday, I took my spot in the back seat. Lexi pulled out on Lizardville Road. We might be a little early, but that was fine with me. Knowing Tom, he would be ready. We would pick Tom up at 10:00 and have him back by 6:00. That gave us eight hours to discuss what happened in the cave and the voices I was hearing.

Lexi pulled under the awning so it would be fewer steps for Tom. My heart skipped a beat as I opened the car door. Sara and Lexi remained in the car. I strolled up to the doors, and they opened. I smiled when I spotted Tom sitting in the waiting area. He gradually rose to his feet. I hugged him. "Great seeing you," I said.

"Get me out of here," Tom said excitedly.

"Mr. Malone, Mr. Malone," the receptionist repeated. "You need to sign this paperwork." She pointed to some papers on her desk. I dashed over and signed them. Tom was mine for the day. I turned, and Tom was already five steps ahead of me.

I opened the car door and helped Tom in the back seat. He smiled and looked back and forth. Our first stop was the general store that Tom used to own. Tom gazed out the window the entire way. I was talking about the good ole days.

Lexi pulled up to the gas pump. A young man bounced out of the store and trotted to her window. I was already out of the vehicle and helping Tom to his feet. I heard the kid ask Lexi if she wanted to fill the tank. She nodded and requested he clean the windshield, too. Tom and I walked toward the store. He paused several times and smiled, and I watched a tear track down the side of his cheek.

The bells rang when we pushed the door open. Tom glanced around. "Not much has changed," he said, patting me on the back. Tom walked toward the office. The bells rang again. "Sir, you can't go back there," the young man announced.

Tom turned around, making eye contact with the young man. "Oh my gosh, it's you!" The kid went speechless. He pointed above Tom's head. I noticed the picture of Tom on the wall with Tom standing directly underneath it. "You're the original owner," the young man said.

"No, that was my parents," Tom said cheerfully. "This is John Malone. He used to work for me," Tom added.

"Wow, you are still friends? That's amazing. I hope Sandy and I are still friends later in life," the boy said.

He gave us free rein in the store. Tom walked about, touching a few things as he walked past. He never stopped smiling. It was great watching him. He was reliving his life before me. What a touching scene.

Tom relished the moment and finally mentioned he was ready to go. We thanked the young man for helping us out. We picked up a pack of Pepsi and a family-size bag of Middleswarth potato chips. Tom tried to pay, but the young man would not allow it. I slipped him a ten for his troubles.

The next stop was the ax factory dam. Once the car rolled to a stop, Tom opened his door and stood just outside, admiring from a distance. I gazed at the mountains and even pointed toward the path leading to the cave. Sara's eyes watered up, and I wasn't far behind. Moments later, we were back on the road and heading to Lexi's house.

When Lexi turned in the driveway, Tom asked her to slow down. He wanted to savor the moment. We cleared the long line of bushes. The field was freshly mowed. I spotted the kids fishing along the bank. Parker and Buck paced back and forth, teaching them. We rolled up next to the front porch. Tom was all smiles. "This place brings back so many great memories," Tom whispered.

I blushed when Sara wrapped her arms around me and said she loved me. This moment was going to be the best part of the trip—helping my friend Tom celebrate his life. We went inside, taking our seats on the couch. I took the opportunity to catch Tom up on what happened two days ago. I led with Jimmy's back, and he was holding the kids hostage in the cave. Tom explained how Jimmy must be feeling.

We chatted about old times and the days working together while Lexi and Sara prepared lunch. I glanced at the food on the counter. There was enough to feed an army. Not to mention the family-size bag of Middleswarth potato chips.

I glanced at Tom. "Can I tell you something?"

"You have shared your life with me, Johnny. Now you ask permission?" He grinned.

"Yeah, you're right." I chuckled lightly. "Before we arrived back in town, I started hearing a voice. It grew stronger when we arrived at Lexi's house. He warned me to stay away. Could this be Bob Smithers?"

"I'm sure it is. If you like, I can call him and ask." Tom twitched his fingers, and his hand shook for a moment.

"Tom, you realize Bob passed away a few years ago?"

"Of course, I know. I went to his funeral. I meant I can summon him here. He comes to visit me at the home, too," Tom said.

I was in shock. "You can do that?"

"Johnny, I developed into a supreme wizard, a master of the dark arts. I only wish my mother was here to watch. That's the one person I can't seem to reach." Tom frowned.

"I'm sure she would be proud of you," I said, and Tom nodded.

"You know, a wizard is just a fancy name for a witch," Tom said. "Let me call Bob. I'm sure he will come," Tom said.

"John, can you call the others inside so we can eat?" Sara said over her shoulder.

"I'll be right back, Tom." *I want to continue this conversation.*

"Sure, honey," I replied to Sara. I shoved the door open and walked to the edge of the porch railing. I leaned over and yelled it was time to eat. They came running like a stampede, piling the fishing gear on the front porch and dashing inside to grab lunch. It was good that I stepped to the side before being run over. I was the last one in and was surprised to see Tom stuffing his face with a large plate of food.

Sara had prepared a plate for Tom and me. *I don't deserve this woman.* I sat next to her on the floor. She always sat cross-legged. If I sat like that, I couldn't stand for a week. After lunch, the younger crowd said they would clean up. Sara and Lexi appreciated the help.

Tom shared stories about his life with everyone. I never knew he and Bob went to the World's Fair in New York, and there were a few other things that I didn't know either. Finally, he asked me if I wanted to call Bob to join us.

Everyone was staring at me, which startled me at first. I guess they figured out what I was up to. I'm glad someone understood. "Yes," I said. "I think we could use his help," I added.

Tom smiled. "Can you close the curtains, please? Yes, all of them," Tom added. Parker and Buck made sure the room was dark. Tom closed his eyes and relaxed. Zack and Amy shot me a creepy look. I nodded and mouthed, "Everything is going to be fine." Claire snuggled next to Lexi, and Sara inched her way to my side. Beth and Daniel looked comfy in the recliner, curious about what Tom would do.

"Whenever you're ready, Tom," I said nervously.

My fingers twitched, and Sara laid her hand on mine to calm me. I was a little on edge myself. I was surprised Tom hadn't requested candles. I guess they were not needed. *After all, he said he was the master!*

"Bob, my old friend," he paused briefly, "I can feel your presence. Why don't you join us?" Tom said.

"Not until they leave," a male voice replied.

My mouth quivered, and I gazed around. Was I the only one who heard his voice? How could that be? Sara rubbed my arm. "Are you alright?" she said softly.

"Don't be stubborn, Bob. You have no enemies here. We're all friends." Tom remained calm, keeping his eyes closed. "Don't make me summon you; please appear of your own free will."

"Stop it!" the voice yelled. "I feel you tugging at my soul. Leave me alone, Tom," the voice said louder. Daniel gazed upward, as did Zack and Claire. I didn't believe I was the only one hearing his voice anymore.

A small blue light manifested in the center of the room, and all eyes fixed on it. "I can't help you, Tom," a voice echoed. I detected a hint of frustration.

"I think you can," Tom said, moving his hands in an odd pattern. The light grew, doubling, tripling in size. All eyes fixed on the dancing orbs. I smiled. Bob Smithers had arrived. I recognized the voice. It was Bob who had been warning me. *I wasn't losing my mind.* I glanced around the room. The kids were amazed. Others like Buck, Parker, and Lexi were content and understanding. The light grew until it became a white vapor, slowly merging to form a person. The temperature dropped, sending a chill over me.

"Mr. Smithers." The words slipped out of my mouth.

He faced me. "I told you not to come here," he snarled. "I even warned you, but just like when you were a child, you didn't listen then, and you're not listening this time." He grew angry.

I grappled with how to respond. I could see through his body. The kids were speechless, almost in shock. I remember how I felt the first few times I saw a ghost. I opened my mouth and closed it.

"Well, boy, are you going to answer me?" His voice was bitter.

"Bob, relax. We mean you no harm," Tom said calmly.

Bob faced Tom. "What do you want, Tom?" Bob sounded tired. "Are you trying to impress everyone with your powers?" Bob pleaded to be left alone. I felt sorry for him. He only wanted privacy, and it was sad. He hovered a few feet off the floor.

"Bob, help me so I can help you," Tom said, still calm and relaxed.

"Help you? How can I help you?" Bob questioned.

"Wouldn't you love to see April and Bobby again?"

"You know I would give anything to see them." Bob's heart softened.

His entire demeanor changed when April and Bobby's names were mentioned. I could see Buck, Parker, and Lexi whispering to each other. "Who're Bobby and April?" Buck mouthed the words to me. Dumbfounded, I glanced at Sara, who nodded. I lightly shook my head, not having a clue who they were.

"When can I see them?" Bob asked.

"In due time." Tom smiled. Bob frowned, almost like he was expecting to see them now. "Do you know where Jimmy's remains are located?" Tom cut right to the point.

"How would I know that?" Bob looked confused by the question. "Is that what this is all about? Helping Jimmy?" His voice rose.

"No, I want to help you both," Tom reassured Bob.

"If I don't know, how can I help?"

"Can you talk to Jimmy?" Tom said.

"He'd likely grow suspicious if I suddenly showed an interest in him. Our interaction was limited to a single conversation after my passing," Bob reflected, noting that it had been a few years since then. "He tends to keep to himself, often residing in the cave where Jacob was found. But you'll likely find him in the house he once called home if he's not there," Bob said.

Everyone was staring at me. I think my boys and their girlfriends realized my stories were true—all of them. Even Ryan seemed startled. My heart sank hearing Bob say he and Jimmy didn't talk. *How will we ever find Jimmy's remains and help him cross over? This is not acceptable. I am running out of ideas. We could leave, return to Philly, and pretend this never happened. We are fine back home; I am not aware of any ghosts.*

I stared at Tom, who had finally opened up to speak with Bob. He was a natural at this paranormal stuff. He was calm and appeared to enjoy talking to those who had passed.

"Wait." Bob rubbed his chin. He floated back and forth. Something was on his mind. "Have you tried asking the puzzle box?" Bob suggested.

"What do you mean, ask the puzzle box?" The question took Tom by surprise, as did I.

"I played with the box once but never knew how to open it. It's a remarkable piece of woodwork and extremely powerful. It has more power than you could ever imagine." Bob beamed with pride.

"I'm confused," Tom said. So was I. *Yes, the puzzle box was exquisite. It led us to the cave. But what does he mean by more powerful than we could have ever imagined?*

"When I passed away, I discovered the puzzle box can help you. It has the power to show you what you desire." Bob seemed accomplished. Yet, from the looks of things, Tom was as confused as I was.

"Let me explain: You ask the puzzle box a question, and it shows you what you want to know," Bob said with a wry smile.

"But I don't remember asking the puzzle box any questions when I opened it the first time," I said. Lexi, Parker, and Buck agreed. We never asked for anything from the box; it just showed us.

"The box understands your desire. You wanted to know, it could feel your question, so it showed you the cave. Which led you to solve the riddle." Bob blinked in and out a few times.

"No, don't go," I pleaded. "Do you know where the box is?" I asked.

"Of course," Bob said, cocking his head to one side and slowly spinning around to see our expressions. It was a little frightening, in a way. His answer took us all by surprise.

"Well, where is it?" I blurted.

"Not so fast, sonny," Bob retorted. "If I tell you, then what do I get in return?"

"I can help you see your family," Tom said, coming to my rescue. Bob's expression quickly changed.

"I thought you buried that at the cemetery next to Jacob's body?" Lexi asked.

Bob clenched his jaw, expressionless. His body still floating a few inches above the floor, his cheeks flushed, his mouth twitched. Tom leaned forward. "I remember you telling us that," Tom said.

"Yes, I lied. The box is in Bobby's room," Bob sneered.

"Who's Bobby?" I asked.

"Bobby was his son," Tom added. "Can you tell us where in Bobby's room?"

"It's in the closet on the left-hand side. About six inches from the floor behind the second board in the wall," Bob groaned. "Thank you for taking good care of my home," Bob told Lexi. Bob began to fade. He turned, giving a final nod to Tom before evaporating.

ELEVEN

I didn't know Bobby was his son. I had heard about the accident. But I didn't know his name. I felt guilty for not knowing. April must have been his wife. There is so much we didn't know about Tom or Bob Smithers. I never took the time to ask questions. I was only concerned with myself. Just like now. How do we send Jimmy to the other side?

I rose to my feet. I asked Lexi, "Do you have a flathead screwdriver and a small hammer?"

"What are you going to do?" Lexi wanted to know.

"I plan to look behind the wall to see if Bob was telling us the truth or if this is another lie!"

"You're not putting a hole in my wall," she said forcefully.

"I can fix any damage. You'll never know we put a hole in the wall," Buck said confidently.

We stared at Lexi. She bowed her head and pointed to the hall closet. "That's where I keep my toolbox," Lexi said with a hint of regret.

We all wanted to know if Bob's assessment of the puzzle box was correct. *Can the box answer our question?* I guess we were about to find out. I rose and walked to the extra bedroom that Bob called Bobby's room. Lexi said Claire was staying there, so it might be a mess. Like I hadn't seen messy bedrooms before. After all, I raised two boys.

I pushed the door open. Stepping over the clothing on the floor, I headed to the closet and slid the door open. Several boxes blocked the left side wall. I grabbed them individually and passed them behind me to Buck and Parker. Once the boxes were out of the way, I crammed into the tight space. Parker turned on a flashlight, which gave me a better view of the area. I noticed this section of the wall was missing the baseboard. That was a good sign. I used the knuckle on my hand and tapped lightly. The wall sounded solid. I moved a few inches to the right and tapped again. I continued this process until the sound changed. A thud that sounded like it was empty. I cocked my head to the side and tapped again. There was something about this spot that felt right.

My heart raced a little with what I might find hidden in the wall. I crouched in the corner of the closet. "Someone should have brought the popcorn," Tom joked. He still had a good sense of humor.

"Can you hand me a flat-tip screwdriver?" I said and extended my hand behind my back. "Any time now," I whispered. I was growing impatient. I finally felt the metal end of the screwdriver thrust in my hand. I placed the flat end into the slot between the boards and pushed. I used the palm of my hand as a hammer and finally pushed it deep enough to get behind the wooden board. I tried pressing the screwdriver to the left and started to pry the board. After a few attempts, it finally moved a little.

I tapped the handle with my fist, and the board made a popping sound. "Don't break the wood," Lexi hollered.

"I'll be careful," I said. I moved the flat tip up a few inches and worked on loosening a different section of the board. I could pry each section farther than the prior spot and finally got a peek inside. I noticed something hidden in the void behind the wall. "I see something!" I shouted.

"What is it?" Sara said.

"I don't know yet, but there is something back here," I added.

I continued prying the board loose, and after the fifth or sixth location, the nails gave way, revealing a six- or seven-inch gap. "Hand me the flashlight," I said, placing my hand behind me. I felt the coldness of the metal in the palm of my hand. I pulled the light before me and shined it inside to get a better look. Something was wrapped in a small washcloth or hand towel and wrapped again with plastic food wrap. Bob had thought of everything to protect the puzzle box from the elements.

I heard whispers behind me and a few objections. "What's that?" I said.

"Nothing. Keep going," Parker said.

I heard more rumbling. I stopped, backed up, and pushed out of the corner to the edge of the closet door. "What's going on?" I repeated. "I heard someone say something about stopping?"

"Dad, I don't think we should do this," Zack said softly.

"What?" I could barely hear and understand what he said.

"I think we should leave things alone and just forget about ghosts. It's freaking us out," Zack said loud and clear this time.

"It's freaking who out?" I replied.

Zack slowly raised his hand. I watched Amy, Beth, and Daniel follow his actions. "Claire? Ryan? Lexi? Anyone else?" Ryan moved his hand and then stopped when Buck shot him an odd look. "Listen, I understand you're a little scared. Me too. But you opened the spirit world when you explored the cave. Now Jimmy is back. We can't just leave and let your aunt Lexi and cousin Claire deal with this," I pleaded my case.

"Your dad's right. If something happened to one of them, I could not live with myself knowing we did nothing to help," Sara said. She had my back, and I was glad she was on board.

"You're willing to risk our lives?" Daniel muttered.

"You started this. All of you." Tom pointed to each kid. "Now, we need to see it through to the end. I know more than you can imagine about spirits. They won't leave you alone. They will haunt you forever," Tom said.

"How can we protect ourselves? They're ghosts," Daniel said nervously.

"Crystals, incense, and salt are powerful tools to ward off evil spirits," Tom mentioned.

I snickered softly and felt the slap of Sara's hand on the back of my head. "Hey, that hurt." I looked at her in surprise.

She knew they didn't help us much when we faced Annabelle in the cemetery. I needed to finish and pull the box from the wall so we could stop all these questions and doubts. Could the puzzle box help us solve this mystery? "Are you okay with me finishing what I started?"

I took the nods as a sign of approval and turned my attention to the closet wall. I inched closer and pried the board back to give me a better view. I pushed my finger behind the package and tried to free it from the two beams it was wedged between. It didn't budge. I worked a second finger into the tight space and pulled harder until I felt it slightly move. I slid the shaft of the screwdriver behind the bundle. I didn't want to damage the box. It needed to remain intact if I wanted the box to answer our questions.

I felt the package was well preserved due to all the wrapping surrounding the wooden box. I lightly jerked the screwdriver forward, and I noticed it moved. I pushed my hand behind the box and freed it from the wall. I smiled and tapped my fingers on the plastic wrap.

"Oh my gosh," I yelled. "It's spewing a deadly mist. Ah, it's burning my flesh," I screamed. I heard screaming and shouting behind me. Boys and girls alike. I had to stop when Sara thumped me on the back of the head.

"That's not funny," Sara said. "They're already scared," she hissed a little. Then gave me a wink.

"That's not funny, Dad," Zack scolded me.

"Dad, you made Beth cry," Daniel added.

"I'm sorry, Beth. I was only trying to lighten the mood," I apologized.

"It's alright, Mr. Malone," Beth said with an evil grin before she started to laugh. "Okay, you got me, and I deserved that." I was glad to see someone with a sense of humor.

The box was back in my hands. I had last held the puzzle box after Jimmy died. He had left it to me. It was Sara and me who first opened the box by accident. Nonetheless, we opened it. I turned the package over and over in my hands. I couldn't wait to unwrap it and see if I remembered it correctly.

I inched my way backward. My right knee seared. The pain shot up my thigh. I was getting too old to be crawling on my hands and knees. Slowly, I backed up until I cleared the closet doorway. I turned to face everyone. I extended my hands out and upward, holding the neatly wrapped puzzle box for all to see. Tom's eyes watered as he smiled. I know this had to bring back some good memories for him.

I glanced at Sara and Lexi. Everyone was fixated on the package as if I were holding the winning million-dollar lottery ticket. I chuckled on the inside. I gazed at Buck, Parker, and Ryan. Everyone was glued to the parcel I was holding. Finally, I looked at Zack, Daniel, Beth, and Amy. They stared at the box, intrigued by the unknown.

My heart warmed, and I was gratified to show my boys that my stories were real, not some made-up childhood fantasy. Every last detail was accurate, from the spirits they now knew were authentic to the puzzle box I was holding in my hands. I planted one foot on the floor and then the other. Sara tucked her hand under my arm to assist. Even the simple task of standing up had become a chore. Getting old was not for the weak.

One by one, the room cleared, and I followed everyone back to Lexi's living room. It's funny how everyone sat in the same place they had before we went to look for the box. Lexi strolled to the kitchen and returned with a small knife. She handed me the knife, handle first for safety. I turned the knife slowly in my fingers and firmly laid the bundle on the coffee table.

"Would anyone like something to drink?" Buck said. He was opening the refrigerator door.

His question caught me off guard. By the others' expressions, I knew I was not the only one who felt this way, but I was a little thirsty. "Yes, I'll take a Pepsi," I said.

Sara shot me her side-eye. But I ignored her as I felt parched. The drink was what I needed to calm my nerves.

"Can you grab me one too? They won't let us drink soda pop in the home," Tom added.

Buck popped two more open, handing one to Tom and then to me. I brought the bottle to my lips and savored the moment. "Ahh." I nodded.

I glanced at the wrapped package and rubbed my hand on my chin as I studied the box. *Where to cut first? I don't want to damage the puzzle box. I need it to show us what we desire. I have several questions I want it to answer.*

"Are you going to open that or not?" Parker said harshly.

I glanced at Parker and nodded. I pulled the box closer to me and slowly worked the knife inward to snip the first piece of tape. I folded back that corner, repeating the process until every piece of tape had been sliced. I peeled back the Saran wrap until it was on the table. Only a cloth hand towel stood between me and something given to me over thirty years ago. I breathed in. Everyone was fixated on the package on the table. My fingers twitched and shook. I wiped my hands on my pants and gently shook them. I extended my hands until I grabbed the corner of the cloth. I slowly lifted it and laid it to the side. I grabbed the other corner and did the same. Bob Smithers did a great job wrapping this to preserve it for now. It was almost like he knew this day would come.

TWELVE

Could Bob have predicted this moment? I brushed the thought from my mind and pulled back the final layer covering the box. My eyes fixed on the table. I let out a sigh. It was just as I remembered it. *Such a beautiful piece of artwork*. Whoever crafted this piece was a true artist. I heard a few gasps as I ignored everyone. I gently brushed my hand over the top. The soft wood gave me goosebumps.

"Dad, it's amazing," Zack muttered as he leaned closer. I heard a few other hushed tones behind me as Tom inched his way over, almost nudging Sara out of his way. His eyes locked on mine, and we both nodded approvingly. My fingers traced the carvings on the top and sides. I eased my hand underneath. I was picking it up and holding it for Tom to see. His smile widened. He shook his head as I tried to hand the box to him and nudged Sara to hold the box close to him. My hand was clammy when I felt the soft touch of Sara's hand graze mine. My smile grew, and I gently placed the box in her palms. Her mouth opened, and panic rose. I noticed her hands quivering as she held the box before Tom.

His frail hands lightly touched the surface. He closed his eyelids and mumbled a few words.

The box appeared to jump into Sara's hand. The boys stepped back while Amy and Beth stood behind them, observing.

"Is it alive?" Lexi said in a hushed tone.

"Kind of," Tom muttered, giving us his wry smile. "The box has feelings. I can feel them racing through me when I lay my hand on top."

"How can a wooden box have feelings?" Daniel questioned.

"Maybe feelings are not the correct word. You see..." Tom paused as his fingers curled into his palm.

"Are you alright, Tom?" I asked.

Tom inhaled, giving me a slight nod. "You see, at one time, the Japanese called them Himitsu-Bako. In America, we call them trick boxes or puzzle boxes. I can tell a powerful witch possessed this puzzle box. She placed a spell on it, cursed if you will. Little did she know she put a gift inside the box, one that defies all logic. It may have been Annabelle's daughter who cast the spell. No—wait. She had help. Someone more powerful than herself.

"She wanted everyone to know what happened to her mother. But something else happened. The box grew and developed a sense that could tell what the person who held the box needed to know. It could somehow show you what you desired," Tom ceased. His fingers twitched as his hand hovered over the parcel.

"How do you know all of this?" Zack questioned.

Tom smiled. "My boy, the box is telling me everything I'm telling you. It's a powerful box. I've never seen or felt anything like it."

"Why didn't you tell me before?" I asked.

"I wasn't powerful enough to sense all of this. Gifts develop with time and practice. As I grew and my senses changed, I had no clue where the box was. I thought Bob buried it in the graveyard on the hill, just as he had said. Now I feel the true power this box holds. It's captivating," Tom said as he gently pushed Sara's hand toward mine.

Sara's face was slightly glazed. She blushed and placed the box in my hand. I never imagined I would be holding this magnificent piece of artwork again.

"Can we touch it?" Zack asked. Then, he lightly traced his fingers over the top of the surface of the box. Zack stepped back, and Amy wrapped her arms around his waist.

"Yeah, me too," Ryan said as he stepped forward. He hesitantly stretched out his hand and let it hover over the box. He leisurely lowered it until his fingers touched the wood. He quickly pulled his hand back. He was moving his fingers as he stared at his palms. "What an odd feeling!" His shoulders trembled while goosebumps broke out on his arms. "I can't describe it…" Ryan paused. "It felt like it was inside me, reading my mind." Ryan quivered.

"Would anyone else like to touch the box?" I asked, my arms outstretched, showing the box before each of them. Now that we had all of this out of the way, it was time for the moment of truth. Could this box show me where Jimmy's remains were? "Are we ready?" I asked.

I was startled as I heard the rustling of a potato chip bag opening. "What are you doing?" My tone was harsh.

"What? I'm hungry," Parker said while Lexi slapped Parker's shoulder. "Dang, sis, do you need to hit me?" Parker snarled.

"We just finished lunch. Try to focus." Lexi pointed to the box as Parker crunched on chips.

I slowly tumbled the puzzle box in my hands. It felt solid, like wood should. I couldn't believe I would roll this on the floor and hope it would spring open as it did in the past. I closed my eyes and repeated in my head. *Where are Jimmy's remains?* I inhaled, held my breath, and exhaled as I gently rotated the box across the floor. It tumbled over a few times and stopped a few feet away. I blinked a few times as I balled my fist—just a lump of wood lying in the middle of the room.

"Is something supposed to happen?" Ryan asked.

"It should spew smoke out of the side. Why isn't that happening?" Parker asked.

"Harder," Tom suggested.

I leaned forward, picking up the box. *Stop coddling the thing and roll it with a little force. Please show me where Jimmy's remains are.* I pulled my arm back and launched it forward, allowing the box to roll over and over. Then it popped, and when the side walls opened, it came to rest in the middle of the room.

"You broke it!" Daniel exclaimed.

"Shush." Sara tapped her index finger on her lips.

I saw a spark and then a twinkle of light before a bit of mist oozed a few inches upward and paused. *Is that it? Maybe it was too old and rusty to help me. Perhaps it doesn't contain the magic Bob and Tom think it does.* I felt confused, and I had high hopes this would solve our problem. Then it happened. Slowly, a long, steady stream of smoke began to rise. *Maybe it only needed time to think? The box baffles me.* We stared at the center of the room as the mist gathered in a ballon-sized ball. The fog continued to spill out of the open section. It was expanding before us.

I checked on the boys and their girlfriends. Everyone appeared mesmerized. I, too, felt the same. The steam rose almost four feet in height, about the same in diameter.

Catching us off guard, the box leaped a few inches off the wooden floor, and we all flinched. Multiple colors whirled around the base and gathered in the center of the cloud. I had witnessed this once before and could not believe it was happening again. "Please work," I whispered. The colors banded together and started to form something. I leaned forward to get a better look. I wasn't the only one.

The colors mixed and danced. It was amazing. I had never seen anything so beautiful. I glanced at Tom, who had a larger-than-life-size smile. I was glad he was here to share this moment. I turned my attention back to the center of the room. I was watching, waiting. A cloudy figure appeared. I moved closer, almost falling off the couch. I caught a glimpse of water flowing at a fast pace. A raft came into view. Bewildered, my jaw dropped as if I was under a spell. I squinted to have a better view of the three-dimensional images before us.

Jimmy was approaching the dam as he and the raft plunged over the broken spillway. I sat fixated, transported back to that day in 1975. Sara eased her arm over my shoulder. Zack and Daniel were glued to my reaction. The Styrofoam raft snapped. I could hear it in my mind. That plunged Jimmy into the water. His arms were flailing, and he was trying to keep his head above the surface. The current was too strong. He slipped beneath. For the first time, I witnessed Jimmy's struggles from underneath.

Lexi cupped her hand over her mouth. A tear tracked down my cheek. Buck gripped the armrest on his chair. I watched potato chips hitting the floor as the bag slid from between Parker's fingers. Jimmy sank deeper into the abyss. His body tossed, turned, and whirled about, arms and legs kicking and thrashing, giving it everything he had to keep his head above the surface.

It was a losing battle. His arms and legs slowed before going limp from exhaustion. His body slammed the rear wall of the dam. It was punishing his now limp body and pressed Jimmy to the rear wall of the concrete structure. I was speechless when Todd appeared, diving into the water, missing Jimmy by several feet. The murky water made visibility difficult.

Todd was pulled back by the rope wrapped around his waist—a second tear dripping from my chin as a new one formed. Jimmy's lifeless body remained pressed tight to the rear wall, inching its way to the shore as he settled on the riverbed. His face turned a light shade of blue. His eyes closed.

"Why?" I mouthed. I was trying to understand why the puzzle needed to show me this. *Does the box want me to feel sorry for Jimmy? I've been riddled with guilt for over thirty years. I don't need to see this.* Jimmy's body rolled and flipped, crawling closer to the shoreline when it slipped under an aperture in the wall.

My hands flicked, and I gazed side to side, searching for the remote control. I needed to hit pause, rewind, and watch again. This wasn't a movie. The box showed me where Jimmy's remains could be found. The vision continued moving slowly. I could see the river bank come into view. His remains couldn't be twenty yards from the water's edge.

The county removed part of the dam but not this section. We should be able to find his remains lodged in the crevice.

The formation started to fizzle and dissolve before us. But it had shared its secret.

THIRTEEN

I let out a sigh and wiped the side of my face. Sara's hand rubbed my back in a circular motion. That helped, but I needed a bit of a distraction from what I witnessed. I wanted to stay strong for my boys. I turned to Tom for guidance. Neither of us said a word. I felt like screaming to ease the pain I was feeling, but Zack and Daniel and their friends sat across from me.

Lexi rose to her feet, breaking my thoughts. She walked down the hallway, suddenly returning with a blue towel, and laid it on the coffee table before us. I knelt, picked up the puzzle box, and closed each opened compartment before placing the box in the center of the towel. Lexi glanced at me. We shared each other's pain.

She folded one side of the towel, covering the box and then the other until it was tucked away in a nice little package. I hoped this would be the last time I saw that box. Part of me knew that was wishful thinking. "I'll put this in the top drawer in the guest room dresser," Lexi said, picking up the towel that contained the box. She disappeared, then returned empty-handed. I didn't know what to say. Like the last time, things were happening fast. This was why I didn't want to come back here. Yet, deep inside, I knew I—or we—had to finish what we started as kids.

"I can do it," Ryan said, breaking the silence.

"No," Buck retorted. "Not a chance."

"I'm a strong swimmer, and you need me. Please let me help," Ryan begged.

"I was on the swim team in high school and college," Claire added. "I can help Ryan. We can do this together." She paused to look at Lexi, who gave a nod of approval.

"We'll be safe. I promise. I have snorkel gear from when I went to Atlantic City," Ryan added. Buck swayed back and forth, trying to make up his mind.

"Tie a rope around us. Claire and I have both swam there in the summer. The water is mild, as the image shows. The image we watched is what it looked like when you were kids." Ryan was convincing.

"I'm not sold on the idea." I turned to Tom, but he kept his mouth shut as he glanced at Buck and Lexi.

"I'm fine with it. I've seen Ryan swim there before," Buck said.

"I'm leaving this up to Claire. I trust her judgment," Lexi said, turning to Claire.

"I'll do it. As Ryan said, we swim there all the time. So, what's the harm?" Claire threw in her two cents.

"Then it's settled." Tom nodded. "You two will swim and do your best to find Jimmy," Tom said. "Oh, can you grab me another Pepsi?" Tom motioned to Parker, who was the closest to the refrigerator. He popped the top on a bottle and handed it to Tom.

Tom took a swig. "That hit the spot," he murmured. "I remember my days in the store with Jimmy. He was such a good worker." Tom changed the subject. "Jimmy was always proud of his accomplishments. I remember this one time," Tom rubbed his chin and chuckled, "Jimmy tried to surprise me. I was sitting in my office working on the inventory sheets when I smelled smoke. I knew he didn't smoke cigarettes or anything else. Then I thought he was burning the trash behind the store. As the smell grew stronger, I started to have my doubts. I stood and looked out the back window, but Jimmy was not beside the burn barrel. The boxes were still piled up. I thought that was odd. I went into the store to see if Jimmy was there, but he wasn't. I looked out front to see an empty lot before opening the side door to the garage.

"My mouth dropped open; I was stunned in disbelief at what I saw. Jimmy had lit several fires on the garage floor. I dashed to the wall, yanked the fire extinguisher off the hook, and sprayed them until the fires were out. At first, I yelled at Jimmy, asking 'What were you thinking?' I wondered if he was insane or had some love for fires. I also remember Bob Smithers telling me not to hire Jimmy because he was a troubled child.

"Jimmy frowned, knowing he had let me down. He said he was trying to burn off the oil stains on the floor. He had put some gas on them to loosen the oil, then grew impatient and decided to burn them off. Jimmy only wanted to do a bang-up job by giving me a spotless floor." Tom grinned. "Great memories."

Jimmy never told me that. I wondered what else he had never mentioned. "Did it work?" I asked.

"Yes and no. I mean it worked. But it took forever to get the burn marks off the floor." Tom laughed. "I never said he was smart, but his heart was in the right place."

I laughed. It was great hearing Tom's stories of the early years at the store. I blushed when he said I was his best employee ever. *The fact that I was a great worker, and we shared the love of books brought us closer.* I smiled. *Here we are today; we are still friends after all these years.*

One by one, the curtains rustled and blew inward. A cold breeze blew around the room, scattering napkins from the table all around the room. I glanced out the front window. It was a calm, warm, early summer type of day. My boys were startled, as many of us were.

"That's not funny, Mr. Smithers," Lexi announced.

"It's not Bob," Tom said with a hint of caution. "Jimmy, is that you?" Tom questioned. "No need to get in an uproar. I was only sharing good memories of you. I meant no dis-respect." Tom held his hands out as a gesture of good faith.

I shivered and laid my hand on Sara's. She pushed into me for comfort. The wind whirled with force; most of us had seen these little tricks before, so I was neither impressed nor scared. Beth and Amy moved cautiously behind the boys. *Will Jimmy try to hurt us?* I pushed the thought to the side.

Jimmy let out a quick yell that made us cover our ears. Once again, it was something that had been done in the past. The lamp turned on, then off, and flickered a few times. The kitchen cabinet doors opened and then slammed, creating a lot of noise, but that's all it was.

"Is that the best you got?" Parker yelled.

He and Parker had this ongoing quarrel since we were kids. If Jimmy had a few tricks up his sleeve, we were about to see them. I felt pressure on my leg, like someone was grabbing me. Sara briefly jumped then stared at me. Tom straightened up and then looked to his left as Parker's feet lifted off the ground, and he soared backward into the recliner, landing on Lexi.

"Get off me!" she screamed. She shoved Parker to the floor. Jimmy's face blinked in and out several times, dancing around Parker's head. Parker swatted back and forth in a pathetic motion. A smile cracked my face.

Jimmy's head floated in the center of the room. He started to inhale. *What is he up to? Is he going to knock us down with a gust of wind?* I waited for Jimmy to exhale, but I felt the oxygen squeeze from my lungs. I was rubbing my hand on my throat. I tried to stay awake. I looked at the others. Sara, the boys, and even Tom suffered from Jimmy's inhale. "Stop it," I forced out.

"Jimmy, this is not the way," Tom choked.

Jimmy exhaled, and air rushed to fill my lungs. Jimmy was bitter. I grappled with why. I had to be missing something. His face rotated in the center of the room. His eyes made contact with each of us. He sent us a message, telling us he was in charge. He had the power to take our lives at any place, any time. I didn't know a spirit could do that. *How can we fight him, knowing he possesses the strength to take our lives? Why is he so angry?* "Jimmy, why are you doing this?" I asked.

His image rocketed back to me. He appeared sad. He was hurting. "You abandoned me," he said cunningly.

"That's preposterous. You chose to stay." I thought back to our last conversation. "You wanted me to help you cross over. Then you changed your mind," I said. It was killing me to say these things to Jimmy, but it was true. He wanted to stay a spirit.

"Jimmy, you can always reach out to me," Tom added.

Jimmy appeared frustrated. He growled and then whirled, tossing things around the room. I caught a lamp seconds before it hit the floor. Jimmy paused, glared at me, and then at Tom. He nodded and smiled, finished with a quick spin, and vanished.

I blinked. A sigh of relief rushed over me. "You okay?" I asked. Sara nodded. I turned to the boys and their friends, Tom, then Buck and Ryan, followed by Lexi, Claire, and Parker. Everyone was fine. I wasn't sure what to make of this new development. *How long was Jimmy in the room? Is he aware of our plan?*

Tom pointed to the clock on the wall. The day had flown by, and it was time to return Tom to the nursing home. Everyone told us to go and get Tom back to the nursing home. I knew the kids were still trying to process everything that happened today. I'd let Uncle Buck handle the questions.

Sara, Lexi, and I walked Tom to the car. We loaded up and started the short trip back to his home. He sat quietly, gazing out the window. I wondered what was going through his mind.

"What ya thinking about?" I nudged Tom.

"Time goes by quickly. One minute, you're a child, then an adult. Enjoy every minute of every day." Tom frowned. "It will all be over before you realize." Tom turned to the window.

"Tom, would you like to join us when we try to find Jimmy's remains?"

"I'll sit this one out. Let me know when it's over," he said over his shoulder.

"Sure thing," I said and bowed my head as the car rolled to a stop.

I watched one of the nurses push a wheelchair to the side of the car. Sara and I climbed out and said our good-byes. I gave Tom a long hug and then helped him into the chair. Sara embraced me as we watched Tom disappear behind the nursing home doors.

The alarm couldn't come quickly enough. After a long night of tossing and turning, morning finally arrived. Sara and I climbed out of bed, met Lexi in the kitchen, and began strategizing our next move. We had been down this road before. Find the remains, take them to the cemetery, bury them, and watch the spirit vanish forever. But not without a fight.

Somehow, I felt this would be different; Jimmy knew our every step. I had to think of something different. Something to throw Jimmy off track. I pondered if there might be a better way.

"What if we have the boys dive and locate the remains? Then we notify the police. They could bring divers to remove the corpse. The police could close an old missing person case. Have a funeral and bury the remains. That would cross Jimmy over, and Jimmy wouldn't dare show up at a public event," I suggested. *Or would he?* "This would also release us from sending Jimmy to the other side," I added.

"I like your plan. Have you considered what happens after they find Jimmy's remains?" Lexi said.

"What am I missing?"

"One, it's not that easy. First, they would take Jimmy to the coroner's office where they would need to do a DNA test to make sure it is his remains. That could take weeks or months." Lexi rolled her eyes. "Then they might even cremate him instead of burying him. Have you considered that?"

"I didn't say my plan was perfect. I'm trying to think outside the box," I said.

"Don't get me wrong. I like the idea. But are you willing to return in a few weeks or months?"

I turned to Sara, looking for support. She glanced at Lexi and then back to me. She clenched her teeth, followed by a frown. "I think we need to locate the remains first. Then decide what the next step should be," Sara said, seeking approval.

"If we find the remains, we should remove them quickly and go to the cemetery," Lexi said. "This offers us the quickest resolution to our problem," she added.

"Maybe we wait and talk to Buck and Parker before we make a final decision," I said.

ZACK

FOURTEEN

Amy and I entered the kitchen to find Mom, Dad, and Aunt Lexi gathered there. They quickly informed us they needed to run over to Uncle Parker's. Despite their casual demeanor, a sense lingered in the air as if they were concealing something from us. I couldn't quite put my finger on it, but an underlying tension left me feeling unsettled.

I quickly gathered the others and decided breakfast could wait. Daniel, Ryan, the girls, and I loaded up and followed Dad's car. Mom and Dad had forgotten that this wasn't just about them. Jimmy had threatened us all. That meant this was everyone's problem, and we all had a say.

Daniel, Ryan, and I had already decided to swim at the dam. Heck, I was shocked that the girls wanted to join us. This was going to be a fun day. There was nothing our parents could say that would stop us. We planned to take turns diving with the snorkeling gear until we found Jimmy's remains if his skeleton was even there.

Who knew if the puzzle box showed us the truth? What if it showed us what we wanted to see? Funnier things have happened. Mom, Dad, and our uncles had a lot to learn. It was time for them to step aside and let us handle things. Maybe we should send them to the cemetery to dig a hole while we swam. That would be the first thing I would like to happen. But they hadn't asked any of us what we thought. They needed to trust us. We were not kids anymore.

I pulled into Uncle Parker's house and parked alongside Dad's car. We opened the doors, grabbed our knapsacks, and headed inside the home. I strolled through the door and embraced Uncle Buck and Parker in a man hug before I set my bag on the floor.

"I have some leftover bacon and eggs on the stove if anyone's hungry," Parker offered.

I shrugged that off while Daniel, Beth, and Claire headed to the kitchen. Ryan and I remained behind, so we had a say in the decisions that our parents were about to make. Dad started with this plan to find the remains and let the authorities handle it from there.

"I think you guys head over to the cemetery, dig us a nice hole, and we start diving!" I said as I pointed to Dad, Buck, and Parker.

"No, you guys are younger. You could dig quicker than us." Uncle Parker frowned at my idea.

"You said it yourself. We're younger, so leave the diving to us, and you guys take turns digging," I said, crossing my arms.

"Mom, I have to agree with Zack," Claire said, appealing to her mother.

"They have a point. You guys go dig the hole and let them handle this," Lexi said firmly.

Mom shot Dad a head nod, who frowned. "Fine," Dad said. "We won't be gone long.

The three of them didn't put up a fight like I had expected. I was stunned. They went out back to grab some gear. It wasn't long before I heard Parker's truck roar to life and fade in the distance. Beth and Amy strolled in wearing bikinis. I guess it was time to get this party started. I darted to the bedroom, stripped, and threw on my swimsuit. I rejoined the group in the living room. Ryan had several pairs of goggles and two equipped with snorkels.

I grabbed some towels and headed out the door. Mom and Aunt Lexi followed close behind. I paused at Lizardville Road and looked both ways while Ryan and Claire walked past me. "You guys should be more careful," I said.

"You have to learn to listen. You'll know if something is coming," Claire said. At the same time, Ryan snickered as he walked down the embankment. I felt a little foolish. I had only heard two or three cars pass all day.

"Are you sure it's safe to swim here? After all, there is a dead body down there!" Amy said, locking her arm around mine. I gave her a brief smile.

"You have a valid point, but this is something we have to do. I don't want to let anyone down. Does that make sense?" I whispered.

Amy nodded reluctantly.

We stepped out on the concrete slab that extended halfway across the creek. I counted off twenty paces, remembering what Dad said about twenty yards. I felt confident we were close. Mom and Lexi opened their foldup chairs. *I guess they are enjoying the time away from the guys. I can't blame them.* Daniel placed a small cooler next to Mom. At the same time, Amy took a place on the edge of the walkway. She dangled her feet over the edge and dipped her toes in as she swirled them in a circular motion.

A splash darted my attention in the other direction. "Whew, the water feels great," Ryan hollered, swimming a few feet away.

"How cold is it?" I asked.

"Maybe sixty or sixty-five?"

"Dang, that's not warm," Daniel yelled back.

"Trust me, it feels fine. Come on in."

I took a few steps and dove in. The initial shock of the cold water woke me up. After a few moments, Ryan was right. It wasn't that bad. Amy tossed me a full face snorkel. I swished the mask in the water, then strapped it over my head. I couldn't wait to see what was under the murky water. I glanced at Ryan, who nodded and then dove. I watched his feet disappear under the water's surface and followed suit. The snorkel gear would allow us two to three minutes underwater before we had to go topside. This was going to take some time.

Visibility wasn't the greatest; I could see five or six feet before me, but that was it. I caught a glimpse of Ryan's feet heading to the bottom. I scissor-kicked a few times, trying to catch up. The current pushed me back. It was stronger than I expected. I thought the bottom was only eight to ten feet deep. I was wrong. I quickly realized I must be about fifteen or twenty feet below the surface. That was another surprise. The deeper I went, the cooler the water became. The bottom came into view, the murky water cutting visibility to two or three feet. I took my final breath. I touched the base of the wall, planted my feet on the river floor, and pushed to the surface. Once I cleared the top, I gasped for air. My lungs filled quickly, and I felt better.

Ryan surfaced next to me and glanced as he swam to the concrete walkway. I looked up at Amy, waiting to greet me. I perched my elbows on the ledge to give my body a rest. My arms felt heavy. The water was more substantial than I expected. *Maybe my dad was right.* Nah, I brushed that thought to the side.

"We need rope," Ryan said.

"I'll get it. Where is it?" Daniel said.

Ryan said something out of earshot, along with being muffled by the sound of the water. Daniel and Beth darted toward the house. Mom smiled, and I gave her a thumbs up. I didn't want to tell her she was right. I spotted a large crow watching us from a tree twenty yards away. I glanced at Ryan and shot him a nod in that direction. He glanced over at it and back to me. I had caught his interest. *Could that be Jimmy?* My mind raced to the stories Dad told us. It was apparent we were being watched. *What will I do if he attacks us?*

"Mom." I nodded in the direction of the tree.

Mom turned to face Lexi and appeared to be chatting about something. I knew she was looking over Lexi's shoulder to see what I was seeing. She finished, then turned back to me and grimaced. That made me feel warm and fuzzy.

"Ignore it, dude," Ryan said.

I heard Beth giggling; I glanced up as they approached. Daniel was carrying a large spool of rope. I was glad to see they were having a good time. I was, too. I wanted to be the one who found the remains. Of course, I've never found human remains before. A shiver traced down my spine while goosebumps rippled across my body.

"Are ya cold?" Daniel said as he tossed the coil of rope on the cement slab.

"Causally turn around and look at the tree you just walked past," I said.

Daniel did as I suggested, giving the illusion he was chatting to Mom. "Dang, I didn't even notice," he said, facing me.

"Didn't notice what?" Beth asked.

"The crow in the tree," Daniel said.

Beth turned to look. "Wow, he's big."

"I know, right?" Daniel added.

"What's it like down there? When do I get a turn?" he asked, turning his attention to the water. A second later, Daniel fell over me, landing in the water.

Beth and Amy laughed as Beth shoved him. I could tell by the look on Daniel's face that he was stunned. I watched him swim to the edge of the slab and extend his hand. Beth reached down and took it. I watched as he pulled Beth into the water. Amy laughed and cannonballed all of us. We splashed around for a bit before Amy wrapped her arms around me. "Be careful down there," she whispered.

Ryan pulled himself up on the slab, grabbed the rope, and walked to the base of the tree while keeping an eye on the crow. He wrapped it around the bottom twice before returning the rope to the water's edge. "I'll dive down and try to find something to tie the other end to."

"I'll be right behind you."

"Look for pieces of rebar that might be sticking out or a broken piece of concrete," Ryan said. "Any place for us to tie the rope to," Ryan added. I gave him a nod, pulled my mask over my face, turned, and dove under the water. I thrust my arms and kicked harder and faster, trying to get to the bottom quickly. Moments later, Ryan and I both surfaced empty-handed. We tried several more times, and Ryan said he found a spot. I grabbed the end of the rope and tagged along. He pointed to a bent piece of rebar. It was perfect, C-shaped and pointed downward to prevent the rope from slipping off.

I tugged the rope and wrapped it around the metal pipe, planted my feet on the base of the wall, and pulled to take out any slack. I wrapped the rope one more time as a safety measure. We left fifteen or twenty feet of extra rope floating in the water. That could be helpful. Ryan gave me the thumbs up, and we both pushed off and headed for the surface.

The girls sat on the edge, dangling their feet in the water. I grabbed Beth's by mistake. She pulled her feet back. I heard her scream as my head cleared the surface. Daniel looked shocked and glared at me.

"Sorry, I thought that was Amy." I laughed.

"I would have kicked you if you did that to me," Amy said, laughing.

I smiled back. Ryan gave me a thumbs-up. "Not bad for a city boy," Ryan said.

"Thanks."

We rested. At the same time, Daniel and Beth dove down to get a look. I was surprised Amy didn't want to see for herself. She had always been adventurous. I remember once the power went out at her parents' house during a storm. She ran outside to play in the rain, so I had to join her. We were soaked and entered through the garage. Then, there was another time at the beach. She was the first to run into the water, even after the flags told us there were rip currents that day. We both loved the boardwalk in New Jersey. I couldn't believe she didn't want to dive down for a look.

Break time was over, and I felt refreshed. Now was the time to focus and find what we came for.

FIFTEEN

Ryan dove first, and I followed close behind. We used the rope as a guide and a way to keep us on the river floor. I planted my feet on the bottom of the left side of the rope while Ryan took the right side. I watched Ryan feeling around the base of the wall. I mimicked what he was doing. We were looking for holes or places where a person could get lodged. That made sense to me. I moved several feet to the left as Ryan faded out of sight. The current grew stronger the farther left I went, making it impossible to remain below. I had to go up and push off. I broke the surface and gazed to the right, realizing Ryan must still be below. I handed the snorkel to Daniel, who quickly went under with it. We were working in shifts to keep from getting exhausted. Ryan popped up and gave his snorkel to Claire.

Dang, what if she finds the remains? Amy will never let me live that down. Honestly, it didn't matter; times have changed, and I would be happy that we completed our mission. *Keep an eye on the prize*, I reminded myself, *like Dad always taught us*. He also said teamwork was essential.

"Mom, does Uncle Parker have an underwater light?" I asked, thinking it might help to see the wall instead of feeling for it.

"I'll be right back," Lexi said as she strolled toward the house.

Daniel surfaced along with Claire. I mentioned the light, and both agreed. We sat patiently for Aunt Lexi to return. Much to my surprise, she showed up with two large camping flashlights. They were heavy-duty and wrapped in clear plastic bags. "That might work." I smiled.

"If the flashlight happens to get wet and gives out, just toss it in the water. I doubt Parker will even notice." She chuckled, a mischievous glint in her eyes. Her laughter masked her reluctance to confess that she had borrowed Parker's equipment.

Poor Uncle Parker. I know all too well what it is like to have a sibling. Oh well, it's time to get back to work. I grabbed one of the lights, and Ryan snatched the other. We dove while switching the lights on. Wow, what a difference the light made. We spotted several more rebar pieces along the bottom, stretched the rope out, and wrapped it around each one, giving us something to hold on to as we made our way left and right. Ryan wanted to switch things up by taking the left. I was happy to oblige.

I wrapped my left hand on the rope, pulling myself toward the shoreline while holding the flashlight in my right. I glanced behind me, and much to my surprise, I spotted Ryan's light dancing about in the water. I turned my attention to the wall. I noticed a crack that opened. It was way more than a crack. It was two to three feet wide and several feet deep. I moved the light inside, pulling back when something moved. My heart quickened. I gripped the light harder and forced myself to take a second look. A school of trout scurried away when I pushed the light inside the crevice. Something else was inside, but I was running out of air and needed to surface.

I pushed off the bottom and scissor-kicked a few times to get topside quicker. I bobbed out of the water, gasping for air. Amy's eyes widened, and Mom looked relieved.

"Dude what took so long? You were making me nervous," Daniel said.

"I found something," I struggled to choke out.

I had everyone's attention now. About eight feet to my right, a crack opened in the remains of the dam. "Look out!" I hollered. Mom and Lexi ducked and fell from their chairs, landing on the concrete slab. *Ouch, that had to hurt.* Amy, Beth, and Claire jumped in the water and bobbed up and down as the large crow swooped down, trying to peck at our heads. Daniel grabbed one of the lawn chairs and started swinging it back and forth to defend himself.

I splashed water at the crow in an effort to drive him away. Nothing fazed the bird. He circled several times, then landed ten feet away to our left. Like a small white tornado, the crow whirled, and then manifested, taking the shape of a boy.

"Jimmy!" I spat out.

"That was fun." He paused to laugh at himself. "You should have seen the look on your faces," Jimmy said while slapping his knee.

Now I understood when Dad said he was amazed every time he saw a ghost in person. My stomach turned, and I felt nauseous. It was impossible, yet Jimmy was right here. I could see through his body. It was fascinating.

Mom stood, marched over, and yelled. "That wasn't funny; look at my knee," she scolded. Jimmy showed empathy when he frowned.

"We grew up together. We're friends," Mom scolded.

I hadn't seen her this upset in forever. The last time she got this angry was when Daniel and I snuck out to attend my senior party the week before high school graduation. I tried beer for the first time; that stuff tasted awful. Mom could tell I had been drinking. It took me forever to regain her trust. I felt horrible.

Mom continued to yell while Lexi joined in. The two of them read Jimmy the riot act. I had never seen a ghost cower down. *You go, Mom!* I was proud of her. She was standing up for us. For the first time, I felt sorry for Jimmy the ghost.

Mom began to calm down as Jimmy sat there watching us float in the water. I'm sure seeing us in the creek brought back bad memories for him. He shot me a smile, almost daring me to find his remains. I felt uneasy. He was a shifty spirit; Dad always said never to trust a ghost. I thought he was up to something. I just couldn't put my finger on it. I left the stones Dad gave me in my pants. Salt wasn't going to work in the water. *Can a spirit come after us in the water? I guess I was about to find out.* I motioned to Ryan, placed my goggles over my eyes and the snorkel in my mouth, and dove. Ryan caught up, and the two of us swam to the opening. I shined my light inward. My heart sank. It was a blob of debris. I was sure I had found Jimmy's remains.

Ryan reached inside, moving a few small branches and a clump of leaves. A few small fish swam before us. *Why*

can't I catch fish when the stream is loaded with them?
Ryan continued to pick at the mound of grass and weeds.
A large chunk floated outward and was whisked away by
the current. My eyes popped, and my mouth fell open. The
water rushed in. I needed to surface, so I planted my feet
and pushed off the bottom. I cleared the surface and gasped
for air. Mom, Lexi, and the others stared at me, including
Jimmy. "It's there," I said, inhaling air and dove downward.
I was eager to pull the remains out and get them top side.
I passed Ryan halfway down as he was heading up for air.

I grabbed the rope and inched my way to our discovery.
I poked the light into the crevice. Yes, just as I thought, I
noticed bones—a ribcage, to be exact. I stuck my hand in,
and *yuck,* it felt squishy, oozing muck between my fingers.
My hand shook as I slowly cleared debris away from the
remains. A second light appeared. Claire pulled up next to
me and smiled at me. She looked impressed with our findings. I pointed, and she pulled on branches and removed
the soot caked around the skull. If we were lucky, we
could remove the entire skeleton in one piece. That was
the goal anyway.

I pointed at my chest and then the surface before
pushing off. I gasped when I broke the surface, taking in
as much oxygen as possible before handing the snorkel to
Daniel. He was eager to get a look as he dove to join Claire.

"Amy, would you like to check it out?" I asked. She
smiled but shook her head. "Okay." I understood. "Beth?"
I offered her my mask. Beth glanced at Amy and grimaced.

"I'll go if you go," Beth told Amy.

"No, I can't," Amy said.

"Please," Beth begged. "You should try it once,"
Beth pleaded.

"You should go. I'm fine with staying here," Amy replied.

"There's nothing to be afraid of," Mom said. "The boys, Lexi, and I are here to protect you," Mom added.

I caught Jimmy nodding out of the corner of my eye. *What is he up to? Why would he want us to find his remains? Something isn't right.* I couldn't wait for Dad to get back.

Claire popped up, and moments later, Daniel surfaced and tossed his gear to Ryan. "I think he's ready to come up," Daniel said excitedly.

"What are we going to put him in?" I asked.

"How about a duffle bag?" Dad said as Parker and Buck approached. I didn't even notice they were back, let alone Dad carrying a black duffle bag that looked older than dirt. Would that even hold Jimmy's remains?

Mom gave Dad a quick hug. They whispered about something that I couldn't make out. I followed Dad's eyes to my left side and noticed Jimmy was gone. I wasn't sure what that meant. Would he be waiting for us under the water? I guess I was about to find out. Ryan gave me the signal, and we donned our gear and dove. We quickly descended and made our way to the site. Ryan slid his hands in first, picking up the rear of the skeleton. I placed mine on what looked to be his shoulders. Ryan blinked twice, and on the third, we both lifted. I was shocked. I expected the remains to be heavy. I wasn't sure why I thought that; I guess it's because people are heavy.

Jimmy was different. He was light and easy to move. We were careful not to break anything. I'm sure his remains were fragile. I placed my right hand under the skull. *I would hate to knock his head off.* I laughed inside at my thoughts. We looked behind us. The coast looked clear. My light blinked a few times, then went out. Ryan nodded.

Everything was alright. We lifted and tried to pull Jimmy out feet first, and then the torso followed by the skull. Ryan's light vanished.

The water was cloudy. I could barely see my hands, let alone Ryan. *Is this Jimmy's doing?* I leaned forward. I guess Ryan was thinking the same thing, and I noticed his gesture to go up. I knew we had to do this simultaneously, or the skeleton could break and fall apart. We knew it was essential to keep Jimmy together. I started to drift upward. Ryan and I were in sync. We were slowly rising to the surface, carrying Jimmy's remains. I suppressed a shiver. My heart raced. I had never accomplished anything like this before. I wanted Daniel, Mom, and Dad to be proud. I could see the light from the surface—only a few more feet. Everything was going as planned.

I gasped for air. Three minutes went by quickly, and I tasted the water rush into my mouth as I cleared the surface. I coughed and gagged, trying to spit water from my mouth. I scissor-kicked to stay afloat. Dad looked concerned. Uncle Buck, too.

Daniel dove in and swam out to greet us. He placed his hands under the midsection. Claire swam over, offering to help. Now, it was getting crowded, but I welcomed the help. The four of us inched our way to the edge of the concrete slab. Dad was amazed. After all these years, we had finally found Jimmy. Now was the hard part: getting him in the bag, to the cemetery, and in the ground, only to watch him evaporate. I felt like I was living in one of Dad's stories. It felt weird yet invigorating. Everyone gathered on the edge. The closer we got, the more I noticed Dad looked exhausted. Had Uncle Buck and Parker made him dig the grave alone? I hoped not. Hands stretched to greet us as we pushed to the edge.

Relief flooded my body. Dad, Parker, and Buck carefully placed their hands under Jimmy's remains, and the pressure was relieved when they hoisted him up and carefully placed Jimmy in the bag. I heard the zipper close. I glanced about. No crows, no Jimmy. Had he worn himself out watching us? Or was he plotting his next move?

JOHN

SIXTEEN

I couldn't have been prouder of Zack and Daniel. Working together with their cousins, they discovered Jimmy's remains. Sara had filled me in on Jimmy's apparition during my absence, shedding light on why he never appeared at the cemetery. I had anticipated changes in Buck and Parker over time, but I was mistaken. It was my digging that provided the hole for Jimmy's burial. Reflecting on this, I couldn't help but feel sympathy for Old Man Smithers, who had dug Jacob's grave and later Annabelle's.

Anxious anticipation filled me as I awaited a closer look at Jimmy's remains. The boys crowded around the concrete area until Jimmy's body was eventually placed alongside the slab. Together, Buck, Parker, and I lifted Jimmy onto the walkway. Water trickled from every angle, and in a startling moment, a small fish wriggled out of one of his eye sockets, catching me off guard. I began picking and pulling at the weeds that clung to Jimmy's remains.

"I can't believe it. After all these years," Buck said, shaking his head slightly.

"I know. It's hard to fathom," Parker said.

"Jimmy, it's time to let you rest, my friend," I said, rubbing my hand on his skull. We picked Jimmy up and slowly placed him inside the duffle bag. I took one last look and then slowly zipped him up. I glanced back and forth—still no sign of Jimmy. The boys and girls climbed out of the water and wrapped towels around themselves to dry.

"How long before we head to the cemetery?" Zack asked.

I looked at the sun. "It must be around four or four-thirty," I replied.

"How do you do that?" Daniel asked, looking at his cell phone, and then flashed his screen in my direction. The phone showed it was 4:32.

"It's survival skills," I said, smiling.

"Our dads taught us when we were young. How do you tell time, hunt, fish, and survive in the wilderness? You guys have no idea. But you are getting better every day," Buck added.

Buck was right. The boys were learning more every day. Maybe coming back to Lizardville was not such a bad idea. We packed up. Buck and I grabbed the duffle bag while Parker grabbed the chairs. We slowly walked towards Parker's house. You would think we didn't have a care in the world when I only wanted to get Jimmy's remains to the cemetery. I was tired and wanted this over with so we could enjoy the rest of our vacation. We still had a few more days, and I thought we could take the boys to Penn's Cave.

Penn's Cave House was a historic American structure used as a hotel from the mid-1800s to the early 1900s. Today, it was part of Penn's Cave and Wildlife Park, located in the next county over. What separated Penn's Cave from all other caverns? It was America's only all-water cavern.

Visitors must take a guided tour entirely by boat. It passed through the mountain and came out on the other side into a lake. Then, visitors returned to where they started. I thought Zack and Daniel would love it, especially after the adventures they had had so far this week.

We crossed Lizardville Road, making our way to Parker's. I pulled the key fob from my pocket and unlocked the trunk. Buck and I carefully placed the duffle bag inside.

The kids scurried inside to freshen up and change clothes. Nobody wanted to go to the cemetery in a swimsuit. I get it. I was feeling pretty chipper. Everything was working out as I had hoped it would. In another hour, Jimmy would be laid to rest. But we needed to be cautious.

I closed the hatch, entered the house, and walked to Buck and Parker. "Do you have another duffle bag?" I asked Parker.

"Yeah. In the basement, I have a few. Whatcha thinking?" Parker questioned.

"Well, to be on the side of caution, I was thinking we stuff some things in another bag, place it in one of the other cars, and take two different routes to the cemetery."

"Why?" Buck asked.

"Everything's perfect. No resistance. No fight. What's Jimmy up to?" I questioned.

"You're overthinking this. I say we load up in two cars and go," Buck said.

"Hold on." Parker paused. "Johnny makes a good point," Parker said.

"Stop calling me Johnny. It's just John."

"Little John has a valid point," Parker said wryly.

I grimaced. "Trust me on this, please."

"Fine," both Buck and Parker agreed.

"Do we get a say?" Zack chimed in, standing with his arms crossed.

"Um, sure." I wasn't sure what else to say.

"Great because we found Jimmy," Ryan stated.

Buck smiled. "Yep, he's just like me."

I could see that Zack was like me and Ryan like my brother. *I'm glad Parker never had kids*. I smiled on the inside at my thought. The girls entered the room. Sara gazed at me like I had done something wrong.

"What?"

"Nothing. Are you guilty of something?" Sara said.

"No, it's just how you looked at me," I said.

"Oh, please. I was thinking 'Here we go again—another trip to the cemetery.' I'm not too fond of that place. I'm sure you understand," Sara said.

I understood how she felt. I was leery of going back there, too. The last time was dangerous. I got hit with a spiritual blast or whatever they call it. It sucked the life out of me. Yet I survived. Why did everything have to come down to the Lizardville Cemetery? That was a great place to lay all unfinished things to rest.

"Well, are we going to stand here all day or load up and get this over with?" Lexi said.

"I'll be right back," Parker said, dashing off. He quickly returned, carrying another duffle bag. This one was in slightly better shape and had an off-green shade.

I grabbed a few pillows from his couch and stuffed them inside to resemble the real one in the back of my car. Zack and Ryan grabbed an end and reached the front door. I opened it cautiously, looked around, and gave a slight nod. The boys darted to the car, opened the trunk, and placed the decoy inside. The girls followed close behind. I watched as the car backed out of the driveway and sped off.

Sara, Lexi, and the rest of us piled into our car, slowly backed up, and started down the road. The kids were going down Lizardville Road, the direct path to the cemetery. We would go the long way down Route 64, backtrack to Lizardville Road, and come in on the opposite side. I wasn't worried about them finding the place. Ryan knew exactly where to go.

I drove through farm country. Red-roofed barns and silos dotted the landscape. Finally, I turned left down an old country dirt road cutting through the fields, just like we did when we were kids. Several minutes later, we appeared on the north side of Lizardville Road. I slowed when the black wrought iron fence came into view. I drove past the cemetery, pulled into the field alongside, and moved to the back near the woods. This was déjà vu. My eyes darted back and forth. The kids should have been here. Sara gripped my arm, my face darkened, and the muscles tightened in my neck.

"Where are they?" Lexi shouted.

"They should have been here before us," Sara spat out.

I threw the car in reverse, backed up, and then slammed the car in drive. I pressed the accelerator, leaving a trail of dirt in my wake as I headed back to the road. I turned right and started back to Parker's house. This time I went the way the kids would have gone. Panic gripped me with each passing moment. I eased my pace so Sara and Lexi could thoroughly scan the embankments near the creek. An unsettling emptiness gnawed at my stomach, but I concealed my fear as best I could. Yet, I couldn't ignore the fear reflected in Sara's eyes. Witnessing her distress pained me deeply. We shared the same urgent question: *Where are the kids?*

ZACK

SEVENTEEN

Ryan backed the car out and pulled onto Lizardville Road. We knew what we had to do; we were only the decoy. *Why would Mom and Dad offer us up as bait?* This baffled me, but I kept my mouth shut. Ryan drove past Grandma and Grandpa's house. I glanced over to see if they might be sitting on the porch. The old country roads were different than the city streets. These two-lane roads twisted and turned. The corners were tight. One mistake and we could end up in a ditch or worse—the creek. We had to pay attention. That's why when Ryan offered to drive, I said okay. He learned to drive on these roads.

The sawmill came into view. I had heard Dad talk about this place time after time. The house located to the right was where Jimmy grew up. I noticed a swing set in the back. Maybe a new family was living there. It was funny how life goes on. Ryan continued past the stone quarry. The place was more extensive than Dad said it was. Of course, that was over thirty years ago. It could have been smaller.

Ryan came to the fork in the road. I spotted the general store. I'd heard many stories about the days when Dad worked there. Many of the books he published were about this place and the spooky stuff that used to happen. Little did the readers know that some of the stories were real. Ryan turned left, following the curvy road along the banks of the big fishing creek—the water trickled slowly. Dad would talk about when they had a lot of rain and how fast the water moved. I would love to see that.

I often wondered what it would be like to float down the creek on a large piece of Styrofoam. What was my dad like as a kid? I heard the stories, but hanging out with him, Uncle Buck, and Parker would have been incredible. The only camping we ever did was in Parker or Lexi's backyard. Never overnight in the woods. Maybe that was something Daniel and I should discuss. It would be an adventure. The car rolled over the old bridge. Dad said they used to swim here and jump off the bridge. *I've never done anything like that. Gee, times have changed.* I spent time reading but mainly watched movies or played video games. It almost seemed like a waste of my time now that I was here looking at what the world offered.

We rolled past the entrance of my cousin Claire's house. I noticed her gaze down the driveway. She had an incredible life, too. Yet she would complain about how there was nothing to do and how things were boring. *Try growing up in the suburbs!* Yes, there were things to do, but we always had to go to the city. Traffic was horrendous, and the crowds were enormous. It would take an hour to go to a ballgame or concert. And it was only twenty miles away.

Here, they could travel twenty miles in twenty minutes or less. How cool was that? Life was different out here. Maybe Amy and I should get married and settle down here in Lizardville. Mom and Dad would disapprove, but it wasn't their decision. Perhaps I could get a job at the university. Our kids would thank Amy and me for offering them a great place to live. I'm sure Uncle Buck could show us how to hunt and fish.

Suddenly, the car jerked to the right and then left. Ryan yelled. We tilted downward. Amy and Beth both let out a bloodcurdling scream, Amy crashing into me. I was glad we were in the back seat. The car bounced, and my head flipped from side to side. My side window cracked. Sounds of crunching metal pierced my ears. I snapped out of my deep thoughts. Were we going to die? The car thrust forward and then back. We came to a halt. I breathed heavily. I looked my body up and down. I was alright. "Amy," I said.

"I'm here," Amy said, panicked.

Ryan turned around. "Is everyone alright?"

"I'm fine," Claire responded.

"Me too," Daniel said.

"Same," Beth said.

Thank goodness we were all alright. I tried to push the door open, but we appeared to be wedged between a few trees. Daniel tried his door with the same results. All the doors were stuck. Branches covered the windows, leaving us with no options for escape.

How far down the embankment had we traveled? Ryan wasn't going fast. So, it couldn't have been too far.

"What happened?" I asked Ryan.

"You're not going to believe me." Ryan shook his head. "I'm sorry, guys," Ryan apologized.

"It's alright, things happen, as Dad always says." It's funny how I was starting to sound like Dad the older I got.

First things first, we were all okay. I had a few bumps and bruises but no major damage to us. The car was another story. I was sure this was going to cost a fortune to fix. *Let's see how Dad reacts to that.*

"Seriously, Ryan, what happened?" Claire said, a hint of anger in her voice.

"Well, you see," Ryan cleared his throat, "a deer jumped out of the woods, and I swerved to miss it. That's when the steering wheel spun out of control." Ryan inhaled. "This may sound crazy, but Jimmy's face flashed on the windshield when the wheel turned. I think he had something to do with this," Ryan said, questioning his actions.

Claire laid her hand on his shoulder. "It's alright. No one's blaming you, right guys?" We all agreed.

We were a mile from the graveyard. Dad had warned us about this. Jimmy definitely didn't want us to bury his remains. What puzzled me was why a spirit would like to stay behind. *Why live alone? That couldn't be fun.* I thought he would want to cross over. I think I would. I pinched Amy. "Ouch, what was that for?" she screamed.

"I'm making sure we are still alive."

"What if we're all dead?" Amy snapped back. I hadn't thought about that.

"Someone always survives. Like in horror movies, you must have a survivor," Beth said.

"This isn't a movie, Beth. We're trapped in a car in the middle of who knows where," Amy blurted.

"Everyone relax. Mom and Dad will find us," I said.

"I hope they find us soon; it will be dark in a few hours. I would hate to be stuck out here all night," Claire said.

I unfastened my seat belt. I turned around and placed my feet on the back window. I pushed with everything I had. Nothing. I pulled my legs tight, then released. I started kicking the window. My legs trembled, but the window didn't budge.

"Nice try, city boy," Ryan snickered. "Let me try," Ryan said, unfastening his seatbelt. He struggled to turn. Space was tight with six of us in the car.

"Watch where you put your hands, country boy," Claire yelled.

That helped to lighten the mood. Ryan removed his hand and mouthed, "I'm sorry." He stretched out over the top, easing his way into the back seat. Amy worked her way toward the front, like two people passing in the night. Our space was cramped. We planned to kick out the rear window and get out of there. This reminded me of playing Twister when we were kids. This time, the stakes were higher. Our lives depended on it. Ryan turned around and leaned back so he could join me, using his feet to push on the rear window.

My mood changed; I knew we could knock the rear window out. We planted our feet and began to push. Dang, it wasn't giving an inch. I couldn't see anything outside. We were deep in the brush. We recoiled our legs and thrust them forward simultaneously. Impact: the window vibrated. It may have loosened a little. We gave it another kick. I think a few more times, and we would be free.

Beth clicked the button, and the side window started to descend. "The driver-side window works," Beth announced.

"No, no, no. Stop!" Ryan yelled. "We can't get out that way. All you're doing is letting in bugs, spiders, or snakes," Ryan said harshly.

The window slid up and closed. "Sorry," Beth said, "I was only trying to help. So, what happens when the back window comes out? Won't you let in bugs, spiders, and snakes?" Beth fired back.

"There's a tree on my side. I don't think we can squeeze past it—especially us guys."

"I'm small. Maybe I can fit in and go for help?" Beth said.

"She's got a point," Daniel mentioned. "It's worth a try."

"That can be plan B," Ryan said.

"Fine, just don't take forever!" Beth fired back. "I want out of here!"

"We all want to get out. Let's keep our cool," I said. Amy snuggled close to me. I took that as her way of approving.

"Well, start kicking then," Claire said.

Ryan and I fired away and kicked, time after time, until I was exhausted. This window was more challenging than I thought, not to mention that my feet were hurting. I could feel each kick up to my knees. The pain seared.

A shiver raced over my body. Amy started rubbing her arms. Daniel, Beth, and even Claire had crossed their arms. "Are you all feeling this?" I referred to the temperature dropping. I received a few nods. Beth hit the switch again to let the front window down, hoping to warm the inside. I raised my eyebrow. *Are we about to have a visitor?*

My eyes darted from window to window. "Close the window!" I hollered. Beth scrambled to find the right button. I watched as the window slid back into place.

"Do you think glass is going to keep me away?" Jimmy's voice echoed in the car. His laughter grew to an unbearable level. The girls covered their ears. Finally, Daniel caved to the pressure.

"Are you afraid to show yourself?" I asked.

Moments later, a white cloud appeared, outlining Jimmy's head. This was odd and wrong on so many levels.

I was staring at a floating head. My heart raced, and my fingers twitched. "I'm here as you wish." Jimmy smiled and chuckled.

"Why did you do this? What's wrong with you?" I said, noticing the car windows fogging on the inside.

Jimmy froze. He faced me, making eye contact. "I'm dead. It doesn't get any worse than that." Jimmy gritted his teeth.

"I didn't mean to upset you." I didn't know what to say. Amy looked to me for help. "We want to help you," I said sincerely.

"You sound like your dad." Jimmy frowned. "He wanted to help, too, but he left. Everybody left. Do you know what it's like to lose everyone you love?" Jimmy shook his head.

I've lost a girlfriend or two in my days, but I would still see them at school. I had never lost a family member, not even Grandma or Grandpa. I had no idea how to respond. Maybe the truth. "Uncle Buck and Parker never left, and neither did Aunt Lexi or Tom," I added.

"They never had anything to do with me—none of them. Life moved on for everyone, except me." Jimmy frowned.

"I'm sorry. I don't know what it's like to lose someone, not someone I loved and cared about," I said sympathetically.

His eyes drooped, and his lips quivered. I guess he appreciated my honesty. He floated a bit longer, checking out the girls, then back to Ryan and me. "Maybe that will change," Jimmy said, spun, and vanished.

The car quickly warmed. Amy hugged me tight, and Beth did the same to Daniel. Ryan extended his arms to Claire.

"Ah, no, we're cousins," Claire said as Ryan laughed.

"Beth, can you open up the side window again?" I asked as the back side window started to move.

"Not that one. It won't go down all the way. The front window." I was precise with my instructions this time.

The rear window rose as the driver's side window descended. I heard water bubbling and knew we must be close to the creek. I was glad the car didn't go in. Mother Nature didn't take a rest. I could hear birds chirping in the distance. Everything sounded peaceful. Yet here we were in a bit of a pickle.

"Do you fit?" I asked.

"Of course, I fit. Are you saying I'm fat?"

Daniel punched me in the arm, then chuckled.

All eyes were fixed on Beth. She rose slightly and cautiously poked her head outside. She extended her arm out to move a few branches. Next, her shoulders twisted and squirmed, but she cleared the window. Finally, her hips and legs disappeared. I breathed a sigh of relief. I heard footsteps on the roof of the car.

"I can see the top of the hill. We're about twenty feet from the top," Beth yelled. "Can you climb up?" Daniel hollered back.

"I'll try," Beth said as her voice faded. The moments passed. "I made it," a faint voice echoed from above. We erupted in cheers. It should not take too long for someone to find us. Maybe we should have started with that instead of bruising my feet.

It seemed like forever, and then someone tapped on the window.

JOHN

EIGHTEEN

exi's shouts echoed from the right side of the road while Sara scoured the left. With each passing moment, my anxiety surged. Where could they be? As I turned the next bend, relief flooded over me at the sight of Beth standing on the roadside, vigorously waving her hands above her head.

I picked up my speed to shorten the wait. She clenched her fist and jumped up and down. I was never so happy to see her. I could tell she felt the same. Now, where were the rest of them? I pulled alongside the road and turned on my four-way flashers.

Sara bounced out of the car, Lexi, Buck, Parker, and me on her heels. I noticed the tread marks on the roadway leading off the road and down the hill. Beth pointed toward the creek. I dashed to the side of the road, glanced down, and then back to Beth. "Is everyone alright?" I asked.

"Yes, just scared." Her voice trembled, and tears traced her cheeks.

Sara embraced her and assured her everything was going to be okay. I overheard something about Jimmy forcing Ryan off the road. He lost control, sending the car off the road and down the embankment.

"We need to call the—" Beth said.

"We can't," I interrupted Beth before she could finish. "We have human remains in our trunk!"

I received a few blank stares. "I'll take Parker home to get his truck," Buck said.

"Fine," I said, tossing him the fob to my car with only the house key attached. He'd better not lose that. The two of them sped off. I knew they would be back in a few minutes. I decided to descend the embankment, driven by the need to reassure everyone that they would be okay. I could see the car had careened off the road from the tire marks on the pavement and plummeted down the embankment about twenty feet. Another ten feet and they would have landed in the water. Luckily, they didn't because this was one of the deep sections of the creek.

Every summer, we spent a bunch of time on the water, day after day, floating down on our makeshift rafts. I'm sure Jimmy knew this section was ten or twelve feet deep. Was Jimmy deliberately trying to harm the kids? Anger surged within me, evident in the flare of my nostrils and the curl of my lip. If this was Jimmy's game, then the gloves were off. I was ready for a fight. No one threatened my family without consequences.

As I approached the car, I noticed movement inside. The windows were fogged up. Why didn't they crack a window to allow fresh air inside? I stepped over part of the bumper and tapped on the side window. I heard Amy and Claire scream.

"It's me," I announced.

"Dad!" Zack yelled from behind the glass. The window opened. I quickly glanced, taking a head count. Everyone was accounted for.

"I'm sorry, Uncle John," Ryan said.

"It's fine," I said, patting his shoulder. "I'm glad everyone is alright." I grabbed the handle and jerked. The door opened a few inches. "Use your feet, and I'll pull," I instructed.

Ryan and Zack did as I asked. I motioned for them to stop, cleared some debris, and signaled to try again. Ryan slammed his feet into the door, and it popped wide open.

"Yes," I celebrated, extending my hand to help Ryan out of the car. Next was Amy, then Zack. Claire scurried over the back seat, not wasting time exiting the car, while Daniel brought up the rear. "Can you help the others climb to the road?" I said. I gave Zack and Daniel a brief hug.

The climb wasn't easy as we all safely returned to the roadway. Sara and Lexi checked the kids from head to toe. There were only a few bumps and some minor scratches. It was nice having two nurses in the family.

Ryan explained what happened when Jimmy appeared. I voiced my concern about Jimmy's motive. Did he try to kill our kids? I think the others were shocked by my accusations. I noticed Parker's pickup approaching and my car shortly after.

"I guess we won't need the rope," Buck said, tossing it back in Parker's truck and going to Ryan.

Parker glanced down the hill as he pulled out his cell phone.

"Who ya calling?" I asked.

"I know a guy with a tow truck. He won't involve the police. Plus, he has a friend who can fix things at a reasonable cost. I'll give him a call later." Parker nodded and smiled.

I would appreciate any help I could get because we couldn't call the police. So I couldn't file an insurance claim for the damage on the car. It was nice having friends and family with connections. That was one of the perks of living in a small town. Everyone knows everyone. It's also hard to keep secrets, but we have managed to do that for over thirty years.

"Why don't we get everyone back to the house and call it a day?" Lexi said.

The boys and their girls started moving toward my car. At the same time, Ryan and Claire headed to Parker's truck.

"Wait!" I yelled. "We have unfinished business," I said, pointing at the rear of my car. Some of them slumped while others grimaced at the task ahead. I felt horrible bringing this to light. We all know we must send Jimmy to the other side, and there is no better time than now, especially after he tried to kill my boys.

"What about my car?" Zack asked.

"I'll wait for my buddy to arrive. Then I'll meet you at the graveyard," Parker replied.

"Then it's settled," I cheered.

"Ah, I hate to point this out, but how will we all fit in one car?" Amy questioned.

I swayed back and forth a bit. Amy had a valid point. How were we all going to go in one car? Thank goodness Parker had the solution.

"Ryan, take my truck. I don't need it while waiting. He can drop me at the graveyard," Parker said, saving me.

I could tell Zack wanted to stay behind and tend to his car. I didn't blame him. But there was nothing he could do to help. I coaxed him into riding with us. He and Amy climbed in the back next to Lexi. The others jumped into Parker's truck. I fired up the engine and drove, heading straight to the cemetery.

I smiled when I checked my rearview mirror to ensure Ryan was close behind. We didn't need any more distractions. The sun was setting, and I hated being in the cemetery at night.

I slowed, flipped my turn signal to the right, pulled along the fence line, and drove slowly to the back. Sara shot me an odd look, probably because I used my signal. I can be a dork sometimes. I came to a stop, and Ryan pulled alongside our car.

The memories flooded my mind. Most of them were nightmares I've tried to forget. Today, I'd share this memory with my boys. Maybe one day they'd tell their children about it. That would warm my heart.

"Are we going to just sit here?" Sara asked.

No time for daydreaming, I opened the car door as we gathered outside.

"What's the plan?" Zack asked.

"We grab the bag, walk over to the hole, drop it inside, and cover it. That should solve our problems." I opened the back of the car and motioned for Zack to grab one end of the bag. I noticed his eye twitching and a slight quiver in his lip. I walked over, placing my arm over his shoulder. "It's going to be alright," I assured him. "I'm nervous too," I said as the blood pumped rapidly through my veins.

Amy and Beth decided to wait in the car. I didn't blame them—this wasn't their fight. Sara stood next to the car to comfort the girls and would be a backup if needed. Lexi placed her hand on my shoulder with Claire by her side.

"We were kids back then; things will be different this time," Lexi said.

Daniel, Buck, and Ryan flanked my left side. *I guess it is now or never*. I inhaled. I gazed over the grounds. We were less than fifty yards away from sending Jimmy to the other side. Everything looked peaceful. Lightning bugs flickered in and out and dotted the landscape. Tombstones leaned to the left while others leaned right. The occasional bat flew over in all sorts of directions. I glanced to the west to watch the last flicker of the sun dip below the ground. Darkness had arrived.

We had left the side gate open to save us some time. I inhaled, held my fingers tight in my palm, and then picked up the end of the bag. Zack swallowed hard, placing his hand on the other end of the bag. I gave a nod as we picked up the bag and started toward the new section of the grave-yard. Buck and Ryan stayed several steps ahead of us in case Jimmy entered the scene.

It was wishful thinking to think Jimmy wouldn't appear unless he wanted to cross over. Daniel stayed next to his brother Zack. I guess that was for comfort. Lexi and Claire were only a few steps behind. Lexi said we were adults. She was right, but so were Old Man Smithers and Tom. Yes, they got the job done but not without a fight. We had salt, incense, and stones in our pockets back then, not to mention we also had Gladys.

Gladys was never touched while the battle raged that day. There was something extra special about her. Tom always told me that. I should have come back when she passed away. It was selfish of me not to. We cleared the gate and walked cautiously toward the Brooker family plot. I paused to look around. The sound of crickets filled the air.

That was a good sign; everything always went silent when trouble arrived.

We pushed forward, only thirty yards to go, and there was still no sign of Jimmy. I was getting the funny feeling that something wasn't right. Why would he let us walk in here and lay his body to rest without a fight? *What am I missing?* We marched forward, the wind whipped about, and a chill set in. I didn't remember them calling for a storm. Goosebumps broke out on my arms. My spine tingled. Lexi and Claire stopped, taking cover behind a large tombstone. *What did they see?* Something caused them to stop. My anxiety level spiked.

Zack and I paused, taking cover behind a row of headstones, kneeling for safety. The grass was slightly damp. I could feel it through my jeans. I could tell Jimmy was present. But where was he hiding? Why hadn't he put up a fight? The show was about to begin. I looked back to the car, making eye contact with Sara, who was watching from a distance. Relief filled me, knowing she was alright.

Lexi motioned, and Zack and I got to our feet and double-stepped toward the Brookers' family plot. I could see my breath in the air. The clouds hurried past, covering the full moon and casting us into darkness. There were no street lights near this cemetery. I listened as silence fell around us. What would Jimmy's first move be? The anticipation was killing me. I spotted the Brooker grave sites and the hole I had dug earlier today in front of Jimmy's tombstone.

Zack tripped over a small grave marker, losing his footing. The bag ripped from my hands and crunched when it hit the ground. I spun around, grabbed the strap, and pulled it beside me. I crawled toward the opening, dragging the bag behind me while staying as low to the ground as possible. I left Zack behind for safety. I poked my head around the final tombstone, eyed the open hole, and watched Jimmy float out of the open hole. I froze in my tracks.

"I won't let you do it!" Jimmy screeched.

I covered my ears as the sound pierced my eardrums. I dropped the duffle bag once again. I wasn't going to let Jimmy win. I reached behind me, grabbed the strap, and threw the bag over my shoulder, tossing it directly into the hole. "Bullseye!" I yelled.

Stunned, Jimmy stopped and focused on me. It looked like he was begging me to stop. I crawled forward, grabbing the shovel I had left in the pile of dirt, and slowly pushed some into the hole. "No, please stop," Jimmy yelled and swirled in a circle around the grave. I moved more dirt into the hole. Jimmy continued to circle, then stopped. "I'm begging you to stop," Jimmy pleaded.

"I'm sorry. It's for the best," I said, pushing more dirt on the bag. A few more scoops and the bag would be covered entirely. I kept pushing dirt. Zack grabbed the other shovel. He stood, taking giant loads of dirt and dumping them into the hole. Jimmy whirled about, talking about some mumbo jumbo I didn't understand. We continued until the hole was filled. I patted it down. I stared at Jimmy as he spiraled downward into the ground and vanished.

"Yes!" I shouted while throwing my arms upward. Zack, Daniel, Buck, Lexi, and Claire celebrated with me. Sara and the others came running to our side. This was over. A ton of weight had been lifted from my shoulders. I laid some of the sod pieces on the top, trying to disguise the newly dug grave. The others continued their celebration, waiting for Parker to arrive.

"Jimmy didn't put up much of a fight?" Buck asked.

"I know. That surprised me." I smiled.

The wind whipped, and the temperature plunged to almost freezing.

"I should win an award for that performance," Jimmy said as he floated upward out of his grave. He slapped his knee and laughed at us. "You should see the look on your face." Jimmy pointed at me.

What happened? Jimmy was still here! How? We did the same thing as last time. We laid his body to rest, so why was he still here? This made no sense at all. Was it Gladys and the chanting? What step did I miss? My body shivered, and my fingers twitched rapidly.

Buck and Ryan dashed over. They paused, giving a weird look at Jimmy and then at me. "How's that possible?" Buck asked.

"I don't know." I was at a loss for words. Jimmy flew around as free as a kite in the wind. He danced and floated about, laughing and making fun of me, Zack, Buck, and Ryan.

"You thought you could send me away? That's hysterical." Jimmy floated about and finally stopped midair. Jimmy looked directly into my eyes. "You all need to watch your back! I'm about to rock your world!" Jimmy said, then vanished before us.

Beth crumpled to the ground. Sara and Lexi gathered at her side. "Is she alright?" Daniel questioned nervously.

"She fainted, but she's going to be alright," Lexi said as Beth sat up.

NINETEEN

My body limp, I slumped, falling backward, landing on the damp grass. I didn't care if my pants got wet. That was the least of my problems. My mouth hung open in disbelief. I missed something, but what? My mind was working overdrive, trying to retrace my steps. Everyone gathered around. Sara, Beth, and Amy joined us around the Brooker family plot. We had the right bag, didn't we? Were all the remains there? Had the boys left some pieces under the water? Would we have to do this all over again? No, I told myself, this wasn't right. This had turned into a nightmare.

"Why is Jimmy still here?" Sara asked.

"I don't have any answers, only questions." I frowned in dismay. The clouds cleared, giving way to a lovely summer night sky. The temperature was restored to the normal mid-seventies. The crescent moon was brighter than expected. "We need to talk to Tom," I blurted. "Gladys sent Annabelle and Donald Thornhill to the other side?" I spoke out loud to myself. The others were dumbfounded like I was. "What was Gladys chanting that day when the others crossed over? We need to talk to Tom," I said.

"Don't beat yourself up, Dad. How would you know this wouldn't work?" Daniel said, trying to comfort me.

"Thanks." I shook my head. "What did I forget?" I said to the group.

"Dang, I missed all the fun," Parker announced his presence as he joined. "Did Jimmy put up a good fight?" Parker gazed at me. "Are you okay?" I detected a hint of concern in his voice. "Why the long face?"

"I'm fine. It's just," I swallowed, "Jimmy played us for fools."

Parker looked confused. "Is he in the ground?" He pointed at the mound of dirt.

"Yes, we buried his remains," I said.

"Alright, it's time to celebrate," he cheered.

The wind whirled as the clouds returned. I felt the temperature rapidly changing. "You never did like me. Now you're happy to see me go," Jimmy said, floating out of the dirt where his remains were buried.

Parker lunged backward, as did most of the others. I didn't flinch. I faced Jimmy eye to eye. "What do you want?" I asked.

"Wow, is that any way to treat a friend?"

"Friends don't try to kill their friends or kids!" My blood boiled.

"You don't understand. I was only playing. It was Ryan who overreacted," Jimmy tried to convince me.

"I'm not buying your story. Just leave me and my family alone." My voice was stern.

"Roger that." Jimmy whirled around and fizzled like someone let the air out of a balloon. He always was a bit on the crazy side. That hadn't changed. But it didn't answer my question. Why was he still here?

"How?" Parker looked dazed like he had too much to drink. He pointed at the pile of dirt, time and time again. "How? I mean, why? He's still here!" Parker said, his voice trembling.

"That's the million-dollar question, and I don't have any answers. But," I raised my finger in the air, "I have some theories."

"Save them for the house; it's chilly, and the mosquitos are starting to bite," Sara said.

I rose, my knees a little weak. I steadied myself and walked with Sara back to the car. The others split into two groups, half with me and the rest in Parker's truck. I couldn't wait to get back to the house and try to figure this puzzle out. I was sure Tom would have answers as to why this didn't work and offer us some suggestions. *I hope*.

I started the car. I checked my mirror, slowly backed up, and placed the car in drive. I drove through the tall grass to the front of Lizardville Cemetery. I looked both ways, just out of a habit, then turned right and started down the road. I glanced in the rearview mirror a few times. Zack and Amy sat quietly. I glanced at Claire, slightly turned, and looked at Lexi and Sara. I could hear a pin drop. The minutes ticked past, and I wondered what we had forgotten.

I hit my turn signal and turned down Lexi's driveway. The house was secluded, giving us the needed space, and it made for a great meeting place. I wondered if I asked Old Man Smithers if he would show. I would try it; what was the worst that could happen? He didn't appear.

We gathered in the house, sitting wherever we could. Parker was hungry, so Lexi pulled out a lot of the leftovers, and before I knew it, Sara shoved a plate of food in front of me. I wasn't hungry until I started eating; suddenly, my plate was empty. I had forgotten all about the time. This day slipped away; we chatted about the day's events while stuffing our faces.

The distraction made me forget all about our failed mission!

I collapsed in bed a little after 11:00, my mind working overtime while I stared at the ceiling. We had no game plan for the future. I hoped to swing by the nursing home and see if Tom could get out or if he had a secluded place to chat. I tucked the sheets around my neck, snuggled my head into the pillow, and closed my eyes.

I had this strange feeling that someone was watching me. My eyes fluttered open, and the room was cast with only the moon's light. I glanced around the empty room. Sara was sleeping soundly next to me. It must be my mind playing tricks on me. I lay on my left side and stared at 1:15 on the clock.

"Johnny," a male voice whispered in my ear. My eyes flew open once again to an empty room. Smithers was going to drive me insane. *Why is he doing this?* I turned, focusing on the ceiling, trying to tell myself not to think.

I heard the voice several times. There was something comforting about the tone of his voice. It was familiar and calming. I had listened to this voice in the past. *Of course, you have. Now, let me get some sleep!* I rolled to my right, tucked the pillow over my head, taking one last look at the clock—1:52. I was never going to get any sleep. That meant

I would be cranky tomorrow, or should I say today. I would be tired and unable to focus on what I needed to think about.

I repeated nothing, nothing, over and over in my head, trying to clear my mind. My mind was finally shutting down for the day. The voice soon returned. I rolled to my stomach, placing the pillow over my head. I wasn't going to lose this battle. I needed to sleep.

I must be dreaming, and someone was pushing my arm with gentle nudges. I was enjoying my dream until I heard Sara's voice. "John, are you awake?"

"I am now," I said, facing her.

"I'm having a hard time sleeping," she whispered.

"Join the club," I said, smiling. "Between the male voice and now you, I'll never fall asleep." I smiled again.

"You heard it too?" Sara looked surprised. "A man calling my name," she added.

"It's Smithers," I blurted softly.

"Why?"

"I have no clue." I rubbed my chin. "Unless he wants to tell us something." I sat up and leaned forward. "Bob Smithers, are you here?" I waited with no response. "Please, Bob, if you have something to say, please tell us now. We need our sleep," I said.

"Tom," the voice said. "See Tom."

"Yes, we will go see Tom," I replied.

A moment passed. "'See Tom?' Was that all you had to say?" I asked.

I lay down, pulling the sheets up while glancing at 2:22. Sara thanked me and rolled to her side. I gazed at the ceiling and closed my eyes, hoping morning would arrive.

The birds were playing on the windowsill again. I was hoping for a few more minutes. I listened as the door swung open. "Wake up, sleepy head," Sara said. I sat up, tucking a pillow behind my back. I noticed the clock read 9:05.

"I had a weird dream last night. I heard a voice," I said.

"It wasn't a dream. He said, 'Tom.'"

"Okay, just making sure."

"Once you are up and ready, we can go to the nursing home." Sara nodded.

"Give me thirty minutes."

I wrapped things up quickly and joined the others in the living room. Lexi asked if I was ready and volunteered to drive. The three of us made our way to the nursing home. Oddly, we only spotted a few cars on the roadway on a weekday. I had lived in the city for too long and was used to traffic jams, which was sad.

The car slowed and rolled into the parking lot. We were just in time to watch them close the rear doors of an ambulance. Lexi pulled to the side, waiting for them to take the slow ride out of the parking lot. Once they passed, she was able to park the car. That must be tough living in a nursing home and meeting new people and watching them get sick, or even worse. I hoped I passed away at home and not in a nursing home. Who was I kidding? Sara or my kids would shove me headfirst into a nursing home. I chuckled.

I closed the door, taking a few steps. "Are you going to lock the car?"

Lexi gave me her evil eye. "Sorry! Forgot: small town," I said. I decided to keep my mouth shut for a little while.

The entry doors opened as we walked into the main lobby. "Hello," the lady behind the counter greeted us.

"Hi, I'm Sara Malone. We are here to see Tom Evans."

She glanced over her ledger and then typed something on her computer. "Did you say Tom Evans?"

"Yes, please," Sara said.

"Do you all have identification?" she asked nicely.

I pulled my driver's license from my wallet and laid it on the counter next to Sara's and Lexi's. She checked them and compared them to the computer files. A weird feeling settled over me. She returned our IDs and requested we wait in a private room next to the lobby. I wasn't sure how to tell Tom we had found the remains, carried them to the graveyard, buried them, and Jimmy was still there.

The minutes ticked away. I glanced at my phone. We had been waiting for over ten minutes. *What is taking so long*? I walked to the door to ask how much longer this would take; I jiggled the doorknob. "It's locked!" I yelled, startled at my findings.

"Why would they lock us in here?" Lexi said.

"Don't ask me. I haven't the faintest idea." Had Tom mentioned our little adventure to someone? Was he talking about a ghost? I sure hope not. They might have the wrong idea about the three of us. I felt my heart in my throat. What were we going to do? The only thing we could do was wait!

We perked up when I heard voices on the other side of the door. The handle turned and in walked a short, stocky man dressed in a suit and tie. He was dressed like a detective. Why would they call the police? That was my first impression. "Sorry about the wait, folks," he said, lightly swaying back and forth. "I'm Benjamin Henry, Chief Nursing Officer," he said, extending his hand to greet us.

I shook his hand, and the ladies did as well. He motioned for us to take a seat, and we all sat on the couch. It was a comfortable couch. "Why did you lock us in here?" Lexi stunned Benjamin with her question.

"I'm so sorry. All the doors lock automatically. You need a key card to enter or exit. That was not our intention. Again, I'm so sorry," Benjamin emphasized. "Can I get any of you something to drink?"

"No thanks. We are here to see Uncle Tom," I said, getting down to business.

Benjamin squirmed in his seat. "Well," he grimaced, "there is no easy way to say this. Your uncle passed away earlier this morning," he said, sounding relieved to have that off his chest.

My knees buckled; Sara let out a whimper and cupped her hands over her mouth as she started to blubber. Lexi welled up as the tears ran down her cheeks. I sat speechless, motionless, stunned as Benjamin pushed a box of facial tissues to the middle of the coffee table.

Sara wrapped her arms around me, burying her head in my shoulder, and cried. Lexi leaned over Sara's back and hugged her. Tom had such an impact on my life. How could he be gone? Benjamin rose to his feet. "I'll give you all a few minutes," he said, propping the door open with a book as he exited the room.

My phone buzzed in my pocket. I glanced down; Buck was asking what was taking so long. I swiped right, not knowing how to respond at this point. None of us saw this coming. The three of us held each other and let out a good cry. We just talked to him two days ago. He seemed pretty healthy for a man in his eighties. My mind whirled. Tom never married and never had any children. I guessed we would stay longer than expected due to Tom's passing.

How will I ever get Jimmy to the other side? I couldn't leave his spirit here to haunt Lexi, Claire, Buck, or Parker. Or worse, what if he went after one of my parents? Or Sara's? I shivered at the thought.

The door nudged open and in walked Benjamin. I sat up, finally over the initial shock of the news. This was a hard pill to swallow. I never saw it coming. Something clicked in my brain. I had to ask one question; it was eating at my insides. "What time did Tom pass away?"

Benjamin looked puzzled by my question as he rose to his feet. "Let me check the chart?" he said, stepping outside. A moment later, he returned carrying a folder. It showed he was pronounced dead at 2:22.

TWENTY

Sara and I stared at each other in silence. Benjamin looked at us as if he had said something wrong. "Can you give us another minute?" I asked. Benjamin nodded and stepped out once again. The minute he cleared the doorway, I said, "That's when we heard the voice."

"You heard it too?" Lexi inquired.

"Yes, so did Sara," I said. *This is a lot to process*. The room slowly spun. I gripped the edge of the couch to steady myself. Everything was off-kilter. I fought the urge to throw up. I couldn't believe Tom was gone. I never got a chance to ask him about Jimmy. *How in the world are we going to solve this now?* I inhaled and exhaled. The room slowed and then stopped.

Benjamin returned once again. He was holding a small white envelope. "John," he said, extending the envelope to me, "this is for you." I pulled the letter from his hand. "I have some other business to attend to. Please leave your phone number at the desk. We will call you once we clean out his room, and you can claim the rest of his possessions.

Take all the time you need. These events are never easy to process." He patted me on the shoulder.

I smiled sadly. Tom had taken the time to write me a letter. I opened the letter. I was thankful it had been sealed. It read:

John,

> *Thank you for being a great friend over the years. I cherish our time together. We shared some great memories. I know it must be hard reading this knowing I'm gone. Keep me close to your heart. As you know, I didn't have any family. I'm leaving all my worldly possessions to you and Sara. Do with them what you will. There isn't much; they are at the Mill Hall storage center on Hilltop Road. Ask for Larry and show him this letter. He's been keeping a few boxes for me at the facility. Goodbye, my friend.*

Love,
Tom

He must have written this some time ago. His penmanship was almost perfect. It was a good thing I knew how to read and write cursive. Who would have thought they would stop teaching that in school? He'd never told me he loved me. I loved him, too. I smiled, only wishing I had come home more often and taken the time to visit him. I wondered what the boxes might contain. Could they help us solve the mystery and send Jimmy's spirit to the other side? I wanted to dash right over there to get the boxes. But

I knew we had other things to tackle first, like letting the rest of the family know about Tom.

So many of my childhood memories were shared with Tom. I folded the letter and placed it back inside the envelope. I noticed a miniature sheet of paper folded in half. I pulled it out and unfolded it; all eyes were on me. I began to read.

"Congrats on finding the prize; get it home and reap the rewards."

"That's it? A riddle?" I was puzzled at first, but it wasn't hard to decipher. "The prize had to be Jimmy's remains. While getting him home would mean burying him, the reward would be Jimmy crossing over." Lexi and Sara nodded their approval. My phone buzzed again. Buck was driving me crazy.

I ripped the phone from my pocket and noticed it was from Zack.

[Zack: Are you and Mom alright?]

[John: Yes, we are fine. Be home shortly.]

"Are we ready?" I asked. They agreed it was time to leave. As Benjamin had requested, I left my name, address, and phone number at the front desk. I wasn't sure what they might find in Tom's room that might help me in this case or be of any value. However, I was curious to find out what was in the boxes at the Mill Hall storage facility. We thanked the staff and walked to Lexi's car, but none of us said anything. The entire situation was unsettling, the realization that everything had changed. Tom, Bob Smithers, even Gladys. Three of the originals that helped send Annabelle and Donald Thornhill to wherever spirits rest were gone. "I wonder if Jimmy had anything to do with Tom's sudden passing?" I whispered.

"What's that?" Sara asked, turning to look at me.

"I wonder if Jimmy had anything to do with this?" I said while Lexi suddenly pulled the car to the side of the road.

"Everyone reacts to things differently, John," Sara said, caressing her hand on my cheek. "It's going to take some time to get over the shock," Sara added.

I grimaced and nodded to agree. She was right. This hurt deep inside like someone had sucker punched me, but time heals all wounds.

"John might be right," Lexi said. The car jolted forward, leaving a trail of dust and dirt behind.

"Lexi," Sara shouted, "what are you doing?"

"Going to the storage facility. I need to see what's in the boxes," Lexi said anxiously. The car hugged every corner and turn on the road.

"Slow down!" I cried out. "It won't do us any good if we crash." Lexi's foot eased off the gas pedal as the car resumed the normal speed limit. I breathed a sigh of relief. She drove past her house, around the bend, and over the bridge, passing the general store on our right. We rolled by Parker's house on our left and the dam to our right. We turned, driving over the final bridge, the last mile, and headed to the storage place.

She turned, rolling to a stop next to the front door. The engine went silent, and Lexi was out the door before I could unfasten my seatbelt. Sara scrambled to catch up. I slung the door open, closed it, and jogged to the front door. The ladies were already inside.

"How can I help you?" a tall man said behind the counter. I could see the name tag he was wearing.

"Hi, Larry," I said casually. His name was embroidered on the plaid flannel shirt he was wearing.

"Well, golly, if it isn't John and Sara Malone!" Larry smiled, pushing his hat up to get a better look. "Oh my gosh, do you remember me? Larry Cooper. We went to school together," he said.

"I sure do. You played football with Todd."

"Yes, I did play football. I miss Todd. He left a few years ago to move to New York. He was following some dream. How have you two been? I heard you moved to Philly and are a writer or something like that." Larry chuckled. I guess he didn't think writing was a real job. "What brings ya here? Do you need a big unit or something on the small side?" Larry asked.

"I came to pick up Tom Evans' boxes." I frowned, handing Larry the letter Tom had left me.

"Oh my," Larry said, reading the letter. "I didn't know he passed away. I'm sorry, guys. I knew you both meant a lot to Tom." Larry frowned. "But hey, he was an awesome storyteller. He always told me about these wild adventures he would go on. I think he read too many books," Larry whispered and chuckled. "Aw, were they your stories? If they were, I can say I read your books." Larry grinned.

"I'm sure some of them were my books." I wasn't sure what stories Larry was referring to, only thankful he didn't think they were true.

"Hot dog!" Larry yelled, slapping the counter. "See that? I read your books. Well, kind of. You know what I mean." He smiled at his accomplishment. "It's great seeing you, too," he said.

"Do you have a few boxes for me? Sorry if that sounded short. We're in kind of a hurry," I urged.

"Oh, yeah, right. Follow me." Larry motioned with his hand. Walking to the front door, he flipped the lock, then turned and headed down the long, dark hallway next to the counter. I was shocked that the ceiling lights automatically came on as we walked under them. Even this tiny town had come into the twenty-first century.

This place was more significant than I expected. I felt like a mouse in a maze. Turn left, right, then left again. We walked down a long corridor that stopped before a standard office door. Larry jingled some keys, then opened the door, and asked us to come in. I was expecting a mess but opened my eyes to a neat and tidy office. Larry stepped behind the desk. He opened a drawer, pulling out another set of keys. Then he turned to the cabinets behind the desk, unlocked them, and slid out the third drawer. He pulled out a small box, slightly larger than a shoe box.

He laid it on the desk, turned, and pulled out a second box, then a third. "That's all of them," Larry said, placing the boxes beside each other. "Are you alright?" Larry asked.

"Yes, I'm fine." I paused. "I guess," I started to say. I hesitated. "I thought the boxes would be bigger? You live your whole life, and this is all that's left. Three little boxes." The boxes were closed and sealed in masking tape. *Leave it to Tom to wrap them like a package.*

I felt empty inside when I ran my hand over the first box. What mysteries would I discover inside? Books or journals? I was hoping for his life's stories so I could share them with the world. I'd even dedicate the books to Tom, Gladys, and Bob.

I was getting ahead of myself. I picked up the first box. It was heavier than I expected. Maybe it was journals. My heart skipped a beat. I set the box back on the desk, grabbing the second, which was much lighter than the third box. I handed one to Lexi and one to Sara. I saved the heavy box for me.

Larry pulled me forward to show me the inside of the small locker. It showed me that he had given me all the contents. He was passionate and professional when it came to his work. "I need you to sign this paperwork stating you picked up the three boxes," Larry said, sliding the clipboard before me.

I glanced at the documents. It contained Tom's name, three boxes, and locker 127. I glanced at the locker, and yep, 127. I moved my finger back and forth until I read every line. I grabbed the ink pen, signed, printed, and dated the document.

"Well, they are all yours," Larry said, grabbing the clipboard.

"Thank you," I said as I wrapped my hands around the heavy box. We made our way back to the front desk. My mind wondered what treasures lay on the inside of these boxes. My phone buzzed a time or two. Then Sara's phone started to buzz.

"Hi," Sara said, answering her phone. "We will be there in a few minutes." She listened. "We had to run a quick errand. I promise we are leaving now," Sara said, placing the phone back in her purse. "They still don't know about Tom," Sara said quietly.

I placed my arm over Sara's shoulder. "Larry, it was great seeing you. I'm sorry it was under these circumstances. I appreciate your help," I said as we said our goodbyes.

Lexi opened the back hatch of the car, and we placed the contents inside. Then, I watched the girls get in and took my place in the back seat. Next stop was the house. My heart sank, knowing this wasn't going to be easy. Although I knew the kids only met Tom a few times over the years, I was pretty sure they were going to be devastated. How to break the news? That was always the tricky part. I wiped my palms on my trousers while biting my bottom lip.

I quietly gazed out the window. I was wondering what Jimmy might be doing at this moment. What an odd thought. Outside was almost eighty degrees. I was baffled as to why it was so cold in the car. I shivered as Lexi pulled to the side of the road. Sara slowly turned her attention to me, her eyes popping, and her fingers twitching on the seat.

She wasn't looking at me. I slowly turned to the left. I pushed back after being caught off guard. "What are you doing here?" The words tumbled out of my mouth.

"Is that any way to treat a friend?" Jimmy's smile turned upside down.

"Friends don't hurt people they love or care about," I barked.

"Why are you here, Jimmy?" Lexi asked, looking in the rearview mirror.

"Why would you want to stay here would be the better question?" Sara added.

"That hurts." Jimmy hung his head. "I miss hanging out with you guys," he said softly. He was surprised by her question. "I came to say I'm sorry to hear about Tom."

My cheeks turned a light shade of red. "I better not find out you had anything to do with his death." I clenched my fist and gritted my teeth.

"Dude, relax. Tom was an old man. It was his time. You must know that I would never hurt him. Tom was a close friend." Jimmy frowned. He seemed put off by my accusation.

"I know he was," I said, feeling sorry for accusing him.

"Thanks," Jimmy murmured to himself. He almost looked at peace with himself.

"Jimmy, we want to help you. How can we do that?" I asked.

"Taking my remains to the graveyard was nice. Now, I'm buried next to my grandma and grandpa. Maybe one day my parents will join me," Jimmy said.

I noticed a little twinkle in his eye. Was that a tear? What was I missing?

"It's great seeing you," I said, smiling and touching his arm. My hand passed through him, sending a shiver through my body down to my feet. "Wow, that was intense." I chuckled.

"It felt funny on my end, too." Jimmy grinned. "I'll see you around."

"Wait!" I was too late. He was gone, and the temperature was restored. I couldn't believe I never noticed him sitting beside me. He could pop in anytime, night or day, in any location. That was scary. I would never have a private moment again until Jimmy was on the other side.

ZACK

TWENTY-ONE

I paced back and forth, focused on my parents. What could be taking them so long? Something was off. I couldn't put my finger on it. My gut told me they were in trouble. I didn't want to alarm the others. I bit my lip to keep my mouth shut. Daniel gave me a slight nod as he headed down the hallway toward the bedroom. I waited a few seconds and then followed. He must have had the same hunch as me.

I stopped and looked at two closed doors—the bathroom on the left and the bedroom on the right. I had to pick one. I turned the knob and entered the bedroom.

"Dang, man, I was beginning to think you missed my signal," Daniel said.

"You feel it, too?" I asked.

"Yep, something isn't right."

"Do you want to go to the nursing home?" I asked.

"I'm sure Amy and Beth will understand," Daniel replied.

"Of course, they would do the same if it were their parents," I whispered.

"I'll head outside, you follow along in five minutes, and we'll go find them," Daniel said, giving me a fist bump. He left the room first. I'm sure he was grabbing Beth and heading outside. It would only be a few minutes before Amy came looking for me. I glanced at my cell phone. Only two minutes had passed. I decided to head back to the living room.

I opened the door and jumped back. I startled Amy as she had spooked me, too. We smiled and shared a laugh. Once our heart rates returned to normal, I briefed her on our plan. She stood tall with her chin held high. I could not be prouder of this girl for agreeing to stand by my side. If we must face a spirit, then we would face it together. We marched down the hallway, through the living room, and out to the front porch.

Beth and Daniel were standing next to the car. They opened the doors and climbed in the rear when they noticed us. We started toward the car. "Where are you heading?" Parker asked, blocking our path to the car. I saw Beth and Daniel hide behind the seat.

"Just walking around the property," I casually mentioned.

"Why do you have the keys to Buck's car in your hand?"

Uncle Parker was observant. I had forgotten I grabbed them off the table and never put them in my pocket. I slightly nodded, knowing he wasn't a fool. This lie had better be good, or he would call me out. An unexpected savior came to my rescue. I spotted Lexi's car coming down the long driveway. It was almost a quarter mile long.

"Hey, they're back!" I cheered. I also felt relieved. They had better have a good explanation of what took them three hours. The car rolled to a stop. Aunt Lexi, Mom, and Dad all got out of the vehicle.

"Come on, love birds," Lexi said, tapping on the side of Buck's car door.

Man, there was no fooling Lexi either. Maybe living in the country heightens the senses. I remembered Dad's old saying: "Always be aware of your surroundings." I could learn a thing or two from all of them.

Dad walked to the car's hatch, opened it, and carried three small boxes past Amy and me into the house. We turned to follow, and Beth and Daniel opened the door and stepped out with slightly red faces. Beth looked away, almost ready to laugh.

She took one for the team. I wouldn't forget that. We gathered in the living room. Uncle Parker was the first one to ask what was for lunch. *Does he ever stop eating?* Dad placed the boxes on the table. He was motioning for all of us to take our seats.

"There's no easy way to say this," Dad said, hesitating. His hands fidgeted, clutching the side of his jeans. He swayed back and forth and took a deep breath. "Tom passed away last night." His eyes welled up, and I stood in disbelief. Amy grabbed my hand and pulled me back to my seat. Mom wrapped her arms around Dad.

My heart sank in my chest. I felt empty. I had met Tom many times, mainly when I was a child. When we became teenagers, we were busy with school activities. We didn't have much spare time to run back to Lizardville. We lived three hours away.

When Daniel and I were eight or nine, I remember that whenever we stopped at the general store, Tom would let us pick out a candy bar. I loved the peppermint patties. That would be the one I would ask for. Tom would hand it to me and say, "Enjoy your round bar." I never thought about it much until I was at college when someone offered me one. I unwrapped it. I took a bite and noticed the candy bar was round. I never told anyone about my discovery. I would have felt a little foolish.

It is amazing how we remember little details about someone when they are gone. I stood, walked over to Dad, and embraced him. Mom and Daniel joined in our group hug. I felt his pain. Parents don't want bad things to happen to their children. It works the same for us. I don't want to see anything happen to them either.

It took a little time for everyone to settle down. We gathered around the coffee table. Dad was staring at the boxes he placed there. Uncle Parker sat in the recliner with a plate full of food. I didn't know how he stayed thin. The man was always eating.

Dad pulled one of the boxes close to him. I watched him trying to peel some of the tape loose with no success. Aunt Lexi handed him a knife from the kitchen. Dad worked on the box like a surgeon cutting open a patient. I wanted to scream: "Just cut it open, will you?" But I refrained. Finally, Dad placed the knife on the table. He pulled the lid up slowly. I leaned forward to get a better look. It looked like books, old books.

It was painful to watch. Why was he taking his time? Was he afraid something was lurking in the box? Then it hit me: there were two more boxes on the table. Uncle Parker had the right idea. I stood, making my way to the kitchen to make myself a plate of food. *There is nothing better than cold chicken. Oh, potato salad, too.* I loaded my plate and made my way back to the couch. Amy gawked at me. "What? I'm hungry." I offered her a piece of chicken.

She snubbed me. I glanced at the box. Dad had removed one of the books. *No, please don't read each one while we watch.* He leafed through the pages, placing the book on the table while picking up the following journal. *That's better. He is picking up speed.* He did this several times until he pulled an envelope on the bottom of the box.

Dad carefully opened the letter. "It's Tom's last will." Dad started to read out loud. He was glancing at the document. He laid it on top of the journals. I guess he knew Tom didn't have anything left to give. Or it was filled with legal mumbo-jumbo. He picked up the knife and started to work on the second box. More journals. Dad mentioned he would read them all later as he pulled them out one at a time and added them to the stack of journals. I was sure he would start reading them tonight. I wonder what stories lay within the pages. Could this be Dad's next book?

Dad looked intently into the box. Something caught his attention. My palms itched with anticipation. Had he found what he was looking for? I leaned forward to get a better look. Amy followed my lead. Was Dad taking his time on purpose? I gripped my thighs, leaning closer to the box. Dad's hand began to rise. It was another book, yet not like the others. The book was more petite and black. He turned it over and then back to the front before opening it.

Dad reached, grabbing one of the brown journals from the stack. He opened it and glanced at the pages. He was comparing the writing. "This one was written by someone else." Dad waved the black book around.

"Let me see," Lexi said, extending her hand. Lexi leafed through the pages and then to the inside back cover. "This could be Gladys's spell book," Lexi said.

Dad cocked his head. "That would make sense. Gladys was Tom's mother," Dad said.

"Do you mind if I read this one?" Lexi asked.

"Of course, I'll start reading these. I'll look for the oldest one first and start there." Dad smiled. I watched as Mom grabbed one of the journals.

"I'll bet we find something in one of these that can help," Mom added.

"Is that everything in the box?" I said, leaning in for a better look. "Wait." Dad picked up a small black cloth bag tied with a fine piece of string. Everything inside was hard and rattled when he turned it over in his hands. He pulled the string and placed his fingers inside to pry open the top. It was rocks, stones of some kind. I watched him pour them on the coffee table. Uncle Buck and Parker sat up. Mom and Dad cracked a smile. Even Aunt Lexi gave a nod. "What's up?" I asked.

"I remember these," Mom said. I thought the others did, too.

"These are the stones Gladys gave us to protect ourselves," Uncle Buck said.

There was one more item at the bottom of the box. Dad picked up a second black pouch. He raised it in the air. Dad said it contained sand or sugar. He pulled the strings and peeked inside. Dad touched the tip of his finger on his tongue to get it wet. Then he dipped his finger inside the bag and raised it to his lips. He shivered. "It tasted bitter. Yuck." He coughed. "It's salt." Dad wrinkled his nose.

"Of course it is," Mom said. "That helps to keep spirits away."

Mom and Dad, as did Lexi, turned their attention back to the books. Uncle Buck and Parker decided to go fishing.

Amy and I decided to go for a walk. Ryan, Claire, Beth, and Daniel decided to join us. After all, I didn't return to Lizardville to sit inside and read books all afternoon.

We walked on the side of Lizardville Road. I kicked a few rocks along the way, thinking I must be walking in the same footsteps as my father. We stopped for a moment at the bridge. Ryan continued chatting about how he and his dad used to swim here. So did my dad. Somehow, his stories always made the bridge appear higher than it was. Ryan pointed to a trail that led into the mountain, saying that was where our dads played when they were kids.

We decided to follow the path. I grabbed Amy's hand as we walked side by side. I was strolling along listening to Mother Nature. This was way different than living in the city. Birds chirped. A rabbit darted here and there. A few spider webs dangled in the trees. We even spotted a couple of deer grazing in the tall grass. The walk was therapeutic, but time slipped by. We followed the path that skirted the banks of Big Fishing Creek. No wonder Mom and Dad loved it here. Most of my childhood was trips to the YMCA, Little League fields, and school.

I glanced at Amy. She smiled as she took in the surroundings. I was thankful for this trip, even with pesky Jimmy trying to ruin everything. I know that was one of Dad's childhood friends. But it was apparent they were no longer friends in Jimmy's eyes. I wonder what changed? Maybe it was all the time alone, or being forgotten by everyone as they moved on. I hoped Mom, Dad, or Lexi found something in one of those books that helped us send Jimmy to a better place.

My legs grew tired after we walked for an hour, if not more. I glanced at my phone—two hours to be exact.

Ryan stopped and pointed to our left. The ax factory dam stretched halfway across the creek. Everything looked different from this side. I spotted Uncle Parker's house in the valley—a mountain on both sides. I snapped a few photos; this would make a fantastic painting. I met a guy in school who was great with art. Maybe he could paint this for me, and I could give it to Mom and Dad for Christmas.

We sat, taking everything in, giving our bodies the break they deserved. A chill ran down my spine. Branches cracked, and leaves rustled in the wind. A roar that sounded more like a freight train came busting out of the woods and was headed directly for us.

I jumped to my feet, pulling Amy behind me. Ryan grabbed a sturdy branch and waved it back and forth, and the large brown bear came to a screeching halt. I knew this was real, not one of Jimmy's tricks. I fell for that once. "I need everyone to raise your hands to appear taller," Ryan yelled—a hint of panic in his voice.

"Why?" Daniel asked.

"Just do it!" I screamed. My heart was racing, and my hands were trembling. I think I knew what Ryan was trying to do: make the bear realize we were more prominent, and he couldn't defeat us. It seemed to be working. The bear backed up, looking for a way out of this fight. I started to yell, mimicking Ryan. The bear continued to back up. A sense of relief rushed through my body. I knew he could lunge forward at any moment. Daniel stepped forward, grabbed a large branch, and tossed it toward the bear. It slowly started to retreat.

My breathing was fast and heavy as I watched the brown bear turn and run in the opposite direction from the path leading back to Aunt Lexi's. Amy wrapped her arms around me, her breath heavy on my neck.

Beth, still stunned, hid behind Daniel, trying to appear brave for the rest of our sakes. Claire and Ryan seemed to enjoy the rush. I felt uneasy. Something wasn't right. The wind whipped again, yet it was calm until we arrived at this location. The chill told me Jimmy must be nearby. "Come out, Jimmy. Show yourself. Unless you're scared?" I hollered.

"Good for you!" Jimmy floated out, clapping his hands. "I thought the bear would send you running and screaming. But Ryan had to save the day." Jimmy smirked.

We went from a bad situation to worse in seconds. Who knew what Jimmy was going to do? *Why does he hate us so much?* I thought it was time to find out. "Why do you enjoy hurting us?" I asked.

"I haven't hurt you." Jimmy pushed back and placed his hands on his hips. "What gave you that idea?"

"Oh, let me see." I tapped my foot. "You trapped us in a cave. You appeared at Lexi's house and tried to suck the air out of our lungs. You forced Ryan to drive off the road until we crashed, and today, you tried to have a brown bear eat us for lunch." I gritted my teeth, slightly turning red in the face.

"Whoa." Jimmy floated back a little. "I didn't trap you in a cave. I only appeared in the cave. I didn't try to suck the life out of you at Lexi's, and I only wanted to say hi that day in the car," Jimmy said calmly.

"And today?" I fired back.

"What about today? I only showed up. How was I to know a bear was here and he would get scared and run at you all?" Jimmy appeared stunned by my accusations. "If you don't like me and want me to leave, just say it." Jimmy crossed his arms.

"Fine. I don't like you and want you to leave!" I barked.

Jimmy smiled. "That's not going to happen." He laughed, spun, and floated upward into the trees. All that remained was a large crow with beady eyes.

"I'm ready to head back," I said.

"Me too," everyone else chimed in in unison.

We walked at a brisk pace. I spotted the large crow several times on the way back to Lexi's. He never made any advances at us, which was a surprise. I guess he was only toying with us now. We came to the bridge, not stopping to look around this time. Our pace quickened the closer we got to Aunt Lexi's. Once her driveway came into view, I noticed the girls started to sprint and yell.

Mom appeared on the porch, followed by Dad, who greeted all of us with hugs.

JOHN

TWENTY-TWO

I wasn't thrilled that Jimmy had attacked the boys again. The fact they had to battle a bear brought back memories of my experience dealing with a bear at our campsite. My frustration level was soaring to new heights. We had to figure this out, but how? Why did Tom leave me the journals? I had read several of them already, but found nothing of use unless I turned them into novels. As exciting as these were, you betcha, I would write these and dedicate the books to Tom, Gladys, and Bob Smithers. Why include Bob? He helped us on many levels and even gave us more than he should have.

We gathered inside, offering some refuge. Even inside, we knew we weren't safe. I asked Lexi if she had found anything in the black book. She smiled, turned to one of the pages, and handed me the spell book. I ran my finger over the page, filling my mind with knowledge. I turned page after page until I realized everyone was staring at me. I'm sure they thought I was possessed. But I was not.

"I guess we will have to call the dead and ask for help?"

Like most of the younger crowd, Zack and Daniel's faces dropped. But Parker and Buck shocked me when they offered to help. "Tell us what we need to do to send Jimmy packing?" Buck said, clenching his fist.

"Tonight," I said boldly. Lexi, Sara, Buck, and Parker all nodded. Slowly, Zack and Daniel gave a worried nod of approval. We needed to craft a plan, and it had to be good. I wasn't sure who would show up if we started calling the spirit world. Could ghosts cross over and return if called? The last person or spirit I wanted to see was Annabelle.

We had been down this road before. Lexi and Sara pulled out candles and salt. Buck and Parker drove to Parker's house to grab a few more candles, even some incense. I emptied the bag with stones and counted them. We were one short. I guess I would have to go without it. Sara didn't need to know. I placed the bag of salt next to Sara's canister of salt. Zack and Amy moved chairs around, forming a large circle in the center of the room. I had a good feeling that this would be epic, yet I was concerned. Anything could happen when you started one of these. Tom had told me about some of the ones Gladys held.

She made her living reading palms and holding seances for widowed wives and husbands who wanted to connect with the ones they lost. I remember one story Tom told me about an older gentleman who lost his wife. Two years had passed since her death. He started dating a younger woman, no less. His new girlfriend believed in the occult. So, he set up a séance.

Tom said Gladys started, and everything was going perfectly. Then, his deceased wife appeared. She was so upset over the younger woman being there with her husband that she lost it and became violent. The wind whirled, tossing everything in the house. Some items even struck the younger woman and her husband. Nothing ever hit Gladys, who said the spirit even thanked her for showing her this before she disappeared. Yet, that didn't pay for the damage to the inside of Gladys's home. That was the last thing I wanted to happen to Lexi's house.

I was eager, yet I had reservations about what we would do. My gut told me everything would be fine. Gladys had plenty of training and experience. Sara, Lexi, and I had only done this a handful of times. As we had learned, nothing ever went as planned. We hustled about, setting everything up the way the book described. Chairs were in a circle, five candles, five incense, and protective stones for everyone, well, almost everyone. That was my secret.

Sara placed a plate of food before me. *Who has time to eat?* I looked around, and everyone was eating. I guess I should eat since they were forcing me. The potato salad was good, and so were the pickled eggs. I took a bite out of my hamburger. Um, it tasted great. I was too busy reading the book to realize Parker and Buck had returned and were now cooking more burgers on the grill. *Dang, have I been studying this book for hours?*

I finished my plate of food. I must have been hungrier than I thought. I walked to the kitchen and tossed the paper plate in the garbage. I gazed out the window and saw the boys, Amy, and Beth were fishing. This was a place I had never fished as a kid. Bob Smithers would have shot us if we had tried.

I watched them having fun. I noticed Beth was reeling in a nice trout. Everything appeared normal—just a group of young adults fishing along the banks of Big Fishing Creek. I walked to the porch and joined Sara on the swing.

The sun started to set behind the mountains. The sound of rippling water and crickets chirping soothed as the bats took their first flight of the evening. Everything was perfect. It was nights like this that I missed living in a small town.

Lightning bugs, as we called them when we were kids, dotted the night sky. Today, they are called fireflies. Buck and Parker cleaned up the grill and put it under the carport Lexi had added to the property. She had done a lot around this place: the addition of an extra room, the carport, and even a pergola to the rear of the house facing the creek. She even added three feet of rocks and dirt to the creek embankment to reduce the chance of flooding.

We wouldn't have to worry about a flood this evening. That was the least of our problems. As I turned my attention to what we were about to do. I watched the boys pack the fishing gear and head toward the house. Parker guided them to the rear to wrap the fish and put them in the freezer. I was hoping before this trip was over, we could have a nice fish fry. We were about to go inside when I noticed a blue car coming down the driveway.

The car rolled to a stop. Benjamin stepped out and gave us a wave. "Sorry, folks. I hate to intrude. Your mom and dad said I could find you here." He stepped to the passenger side and pulled out a medium-sized box. I was right to assume it was the rest of Tom's belongings. Benjamin mentioned Tom's services were being held in three days. That was nice of him, and we planned to attend. He said his hellos and goodbyes all in one shot. He handed me the box to explore. I held it tight to my chest. Once his car was out of sight, I opened the package. Thank goodness they donated or destroyed the clothing.

I rummaged through the box. It held several knick-knacks from places Tom had visited: Pittsburg, Philly, Cleveland, and New York. I felt a little sorry for Tom. He hadn't visited many places in his life, unlike Sara and me; we had been to five different countries already.

I continued to peruse through the box. I came across an odd-looking ring. It had a large, thick silver band with triangle shapes on each corner and side, encasing a dark red hexagon crystal. I stared at the stone. It appeared to swirl and move in a circular motion. I shook my head and blinked a few times. *I didn't just see that, did I?* I gazed again. There was no movement this time. Okay, my mind was playing tricks on me. This must be Tom's wizard ring. Did the ring contain power? I held the ring up for all to see. Wow, Tom had some fat fingers. The ring was wider than any of my fingers. I slid it over my finger to see how large it was. I let go, and the ring spun to the underside of my finger. I straightened it up when the oddest thing happened. The ring resized itself, fitting perfectly to my finger. The ring must contain power. Why hadn't Tom ever mentioned the ring before? I didn't ever remember seeing him wear this ring or any other, for that matter. I'd bet that with the power this ring held, I could defeat Jimmy. *But how does it work?* Maybe the answer is in the black book, or the puzzle box can show me.

I brought the ring to my lips. "How do you work?" I whispered. I stared and waited. I was hoping this would be easy. But from the looks of things, it wouldn't tell me how it worked. Lexi started flipping the pages in the black book.

"Wait," she said, turning back one page—to the ring. "The wearer of the ring is provided with powers that help them defend themselves against evil spirits," Lexi read for all of us to hear.

"Who wants to wear the ring?" I asked. I wanted to offer in case someone else wanted it, hoping Buck or Parker would step up and feel better suited to wearing the ring. I looked around the room. All fingers were pointed at me. Well, that didn't go as planned. I was hoping for a volunteer.

"You were Jimmy's best friend," Sara said, frowning. I guess that made me the logical choice.

"Alright then, I'll vaporize you all," I said jokingly, extending my arm and waving it back and forth. Amy dashed behind Zack while Beth ducked behind Daniel. I was only trying to lighten the mood.

"Uncle John," Claire lightly punched me in the arm, "you'll have to do better than that to scare me."

I shot her a nod, watching Lexi and Sara clear the room, clear the kitchen table, and put the food back in the refrigerator. The boys helped while the girls helped me arrange the chairs in a perfect circle. Buck and Parker closed the curtains. Claire helped her mom light the candles and incense. I flipped through the pages, stopping at the bookmark and staring at the words on the page. My heart began to race. What was I about to do? I felt uncomfortable without guidance from Tom.

"We're gathered here today—" I was interrupted by Sara.

"John." Sara gave me a look, the one guys get when they've done something wrong.

"Sorry." I lowered my head. I wasn't sure how to start the séance, but I thought about it. "Tonight, we call to the spirits in this house." I paused.

"Should we close our eyes or hold hands?" Lexi interrupted.

I glanced at the pages in the book and turned the first page, skimming the instructions. We faced the center of the room. "We gather today to summon you, Bob Smithers," I said, while Parker turned off the last light in the room.

The candles flickered, sending ripples around the room. The smell of incense filled the air. Peering at the center of the room, I focused on what I needed to do. "Mr. Smithers, please show yourself. We invite you to talk with us tonight," I repeated, awaiting some response or sign. Time passed, and I sensed everyone was ready to throw in the towel. Desperate times called for desperate measures. I raised my hand, pointing the ring to the heavens. "Bob Smithers, I summon you to your residence," I repeated a few times. I was ready to stop when a flicker of light appeared before us. I bit my lip. Others leaned forward—a lump formed in my throat. The light grew. *This better be Bob Smithers.* "Please show yourself, Bob. We await your arrival."

I pointed the ring skyward again, inviting Bob to join us. The light grew. I continued to whisper my invitation. A small cloud formed, taking on a human figure. A slight breeze circled the room, and a chill filled the air. The larger the cloud grew, the colder the room became.

"I'm not very good at this," a man's voice echoed.

I leaned forward in surprise. "Tom," I stuttered. My cheekbones lifted, baring my pearly whites. "Is that you, Tom?" I wanted to jump up and down in joy. When a second cloud formed and started to take shape, it sparkled, rapidly forming into a human-sized spirit.

"For crying out loud, Tom, what's taking so long?" Bob Smithers hollered, watching Tom fade in and out. I hadn't summoned one, but two apparitions on my first attempt at a séance. Goosebumps broke out on my arms, and I could see my breath mist in the air. I smiled, yet my hands trembled. Finally, Tom came into focus, floating at Bob's side.

"It's good to see you," Tom said, looking directly at me. "Oh look, he's wearing my ring!" Tom tried to slap Bob's arm. I watched it pass through.

"Stop that," Bob snickered. "Rookie ghost." Bob smiled at me.

"You two look happy," I said. Tom flickered in and out.

"Be quick," Bob stated. "Tom can't stay long, so how can we help you?"

"What's keeping Jimmy from crossing over?" I asked.

Bob frowned, turning to Tom. "Any idea?"

Tom made eye contact with me. "I wish I had an answer for you." Tom frowned. "I know someone who can help. Mom," Tom whispered to himself. "Mom, please help us. I mean, we need your help," Tom repeated.

Was Gladys going to show up? I couldn't believe Tom and Bob were both here. I watched as Tom flickered in and out and then vanished. "Where'd he go?" I hollered.

"He's fine; he doesn't have the strength to appear as long as me or Gladys." Bob sneered like he was better than Tom.

"Why are you all still here?" I asked, confused as to what was keeping them earthbound.

"Our mission isn't finished. All of us want to close the spiritual window. But first, we need to find out how to enter before it closes. That's what's keeping us here," Bob said, frowning as he slumped forward.

"I'll do some digging to see what I can find out," I said.

"Sit up straight and pull yourself together," Gladys said as she floated downward through the ceiling, sparkling like a supreme being.

"Wow, what an entrance," I whispered. I don't care how often I'd seen this or had a ghostly encounter; this blew my mind. "Hi, Gladys," I said, my voice faint—a lump formed in my throat. I glance around the room. The others appeared frozen in time. I wondered if they were seeing what I was seeing, or was I the only one?

"Think, my boy, think back to the last words Jimmy spoke to you." Gladys smiled. "There's one thing I know about spirits; they drop hints about what keeps them earthbound. He may have given you a clue that you overlooked. Many spirits can't hold their tongue," Gladys said. At the same time, she wrapped her arm around Bob. "It's time for us to leave these folks alone," Gladys said, and with a nod of her head, she and Bob disappeared.

Gladys had the power over other spirits if that was the case. *Then why doesn't she send Jimmy to the other side? Maybe,* I thought, rubbing my chin, *other spirits cannot force each other to cross over. This whole spirit thing puzzles me. The more I know, the less I know.*

I thought about what Gladys said. I wasn't sure that clue was enough to help.

TWENTY-THREE

"**A**re you alright?" Sara said, startling me as she tapped my arm.

"Of course. Are you?" I asked.

"Yes, I could hear everything Gladys said but couldn't move," Sara explained.

That answered one of my questions. My eyes roamed back and forth. The others were stunned, like Sara. "What did she mean by recalling the last words Jimmy said to me? Did Jimmy leave me a clue?" I said, realizing I wasn't fond of puzzles or riddles. I turned to everyone and shrugged my shoulders. "Any clue?"

Zack opened his mouth and then closed it. Did he have the answer? "If you know something, now's the time to share," I directed my question to Zack.

He tilted his head slightly and fidgeted a bit. "I don't know," he said.

"Any clue could help. If you think of something, please share it. That goes for everyone. If you think of anything, no matter how big or small it is, please share it." I paused. "What might seem like nothing to you could spark a thought in someone else, and we need all of us to crack this puzzle," I said.

I also wanted to help Tom, Bob, and Gladys reach the other side, but that would have to wait until we solved this riddle.

"Jimmy said he didn't want to hurt us," Claire offered.

"Then why send a bear after us, not once but twice?" Daniel said.

"Technically, Jimmy only appeared in the cave as a bear. He didn't attack us," Beth said.

"How do you explain the car accident?" Amy asked, sounding coy.

"What are we missing?" I said out loud as I covered my face with my hands. "Grr," I growled lightly.

"Jimmy said you all abandoned him, left him here, and went on with your lives," Claire said.

"What else were we to do? We grew up and became adults. I fell in love and experienced heartbreak and pain. We had to get jobs and care for ourselves; now, we care for our parents. What does Jimmy know about any of that? Being an adult is hard. I would much rather be a kid again. Life was easier," Parker finished his rant.

"I agree with that. I love Ryan, but it's not easy raising a son when your wife leaves you." Buck swallowed hard, his eyes squinting, almost watering.

"I'm sorry," Lexi said, rubbing Buck's shoulder.

"You did a great job. I love you too." Ryan smiled.

"Life hasn't been easy for Jimmy either," Sara mentioned. "Our lives moved forward; Jimmy is stuck in 1975. Times have changed around him, but does he understand? I'm not sure he can fully understand what it's like being in our shoes, just like we can't imagine what it's like being a ghost," Sara said compassionately.

I softly clapped my hands. "Everyone's making valid points. But what's keeping Jimmy here?" I said, rolling my eyes. I crossed my arms, leaned back in the chair, and closed my eyes, trying to focus on the conversations Jimmy and I had earlier on this trip. I was drawing a blank. My mind recalled the last time I saw Jimmy in 1976, and there was still nothing. This was going to be another sleepless night.

"Is anyone hungry?" Parker asked.

We laughed and snickered. "Is that all you think about?" Zack chuckled.

"Food helps me think," Parker added.

"How do you stay in good shape?" Beth asked.

"I walk daily and climb mountains in rain and snow. Nothing stops me. I love the woods. They are peaceful and offer me solace." Parker gazed at the ceiling.

After all this chatter, we still had no answers. I was sure it was something easy or stupid that we missed. I was sure that when we placed his remains in the ground, we would have said goodbye to Jimmy forever. I shook my head in frustration. "Do you have any ice cream?" I asked.

"Now we're talking," Parker said as he made his way to the freezer. "Yes, who wants an ice cream sandwich?"

"Hey, those are for Claire and me," Lexi said, surprised Parker offered her ice cream.

"It's fine, Mom," Claire said.

"I'll buy you more." Parker smiled.

"I'm not going to hold my breath." Lexi chuckled.

"That's it! Jimmy sucked the air out of the room."

"And?" Zack asked.

"I don't know where I was going with that." I smiled and slightly stuck my tongue out while my face turned a few shades of red.

"Have an ice cream sandwich." Parker laughed, extending his hand to mine.

The sandwich was cold to the touch. My mind raced. Every time a spirit showed itself, the temperature dropped. I unwrapped the ice cream and took my first bite. Aah, that tasted delicious. It had been a few months since I had ice cream. I didn't make it a habit to eat ice cream during winter, but summer was here, and that changed everything. This was refreshing. The room was silent for the first time in a while.

I sank back into the sofa. Sara snuggled into me. We needed to find a way to spend more time together like this. The kids were grown and living independently, so I wasn't sure why we didn't. I'd focus on that when we got back to Philadelphia. It was excellent spending time with family. *No TV, nothing but family time.*

Zack broke the silence. "Do you guys remember when Jimmy appeared in the car the other day, and we crashed?"

"How can we forget?" Daniel chuckled. At the same time, Zack received a few odd stares.

"Jimmy said something to us in the car before Beth went topside. Do any of you remember?" Zack asked.

"He said he wasn't trying to hurt us," Amy mentioned.

"No, he said your mom and dad left him," Beth added.

"Not exactly. He said *all* our parents left him," Ryan said.

"No, he didn't. He said *everybody* left him," Claire added her two cents to the story.

"Dad," Zack smiled at me. "Jimmy said everybody left him." I let that sink in, but I wasn't making any connections.

"Jimmy said everybody left him. Do you know what it's like to lose everyone you love?" Zack repeated, adding to what Jimmy told him.

I rubbed my chin, my mind working overtime. "That's it! You're a genius!"

Parker and Buck looked confused. I wasn't sure Sara or Lexi had made the connection either. Zack and Ryan nodded and murmured something out of earshot to the girls.

"I think I understand what you're saying. Do you know what it's like to lose everyone you love?" Daniel said.

"Yes, we heard him. But what am I missing?" Parker asked.

"Jimmy didn't just lose us after he drowned," I said.

Lexi's eyes grew wide, and Sara smiled. I think everyone was coming to the same conclusion I had.

"You could be on to something, Zack." It was a proud father moment.

Parker and Buck were puzzled. I needed to help them a little. "Remember when Jimmy drowned? His parents stopped by the house and left me the puzzle box. They put their house on the market and moved away. Jimmy lost us and his mom and dad all at the same time. I'll bet he is missing them," I said, frowning.

"Maybe he wants to see his parents and say goodbye. If we can arrange that, maybe he'll cross over!" I said, beaming with pride.

"You're welcome." Parker showed his teeth. "I told you all we needed was a little food, and we could solve this."

It was a long shot, but that was all we had. Besides, I didn't want to argue, so I nodded, letting Parker have his five seconds of fame. *Now, for the hard part, how do we find Jimmy's parents?* Heck, I didn't remember their first names. I pulled my phone from my pocket—Lizardville Brooker family. A few searches appeared.

I guessed a dozen Brooker families had to live in the area. Where to start? I scratched my head. Sara watched over my shoulder. I was coming up with nothing but dead ends.

"Try searching Jimmy's name, the boy who drowned in fishing creek in 1975," Sara said.

I turned and kissed her on the cheek. "You're a genius."

I did just that. The headline read, *"Boy drowns in fishing creek while swimming near the dam."* To read the full article, I needed to subscribe to the *"Express"* newspaper. *What a load of crap.* I didn't want to pay to find out Jimmy's parents' first names.

"What's wrong?" Lexi asked, reading the puzzled look on my face.

"I found the article from 1975, but to read the story, I have to subscribe to the newspaper," I responded.

"Not a problem," Lexi said, handing me her phone. "Just click the *'Express'* app on the front screen," Lexi mentioned. I shot Lexi my evil eye.

"Don't judge me. There's not much to do around here," Lexi said with a straight face.

Everyone leaned forward to get a better look. I pressed the icon, and the paper came to life on the screen. I typed, "boy drowns in fishing creek in 1975." The entire article appeared. I scrolled down to where it said his parents had survived him: David and Linda Brooker of Lizardville. "David and Linda Brooker." I paused. All eyes were on me. "That was much easier than the microfiche or old newspapers at the library that we had to use as kids."

I continued my search. There were two sets of Dave and Linda Brookers. I was a little nervous because the dates listed were several years old. "It looks like we're heading to Renovo and then Blanchard." I visited both places when I was a child. Neither town was massive. Renovo was the farthest away, so I'd start tomorrow by heading to Blanchard.

There wasn't anything we could do this evening. Parker insisted we call them, but I wasn't about to contact someone at 9:00 at night and say, "Hi, did you have a son named Jimmy?" There were three questions that we needed to answer once we located them. Would they believe our story? Would they help us? Was this the reason Jimmy didn't cross over? Okay, maybe a fourth question: Would this work?

TWENTY-FOUR

Another day was about to begin. I squinted a few times and rolled over. Sara cuddled next to me. Her back pressed next to mine. I was glad I didn't wake her and stunned that I was awake before her. I felt refreshed, ready to tackle the day. I squeezed out of bed, doing my best not to disturb Sara. She always did that for me. I was eager to get on the road and see if one of these couples was Jimmy's parents. My heart was already racing. I had a good feeling about this. I was sure we were on the right path to solving everything, thanks to Gladys for steering us in the right direction.

Of course, there was always a chance that getting Jimmy reunited with his parents would backfire. But it was worth the risk. Plus, if I were a parent who had lost a child, I would want to see them, even if they were a spirit. I was sure I could produce Jimmy. After all, I had the ring. The ring brought Tom, Bob, and Gladys here last night. Maybe it was their willingness to be here. I didn't know, and I didn't care. We had to try.

I finished getting ready. Then I walked to the kitchen where Zack and Amy were sitting. "Amy made breakfast if you want some scrambled eggs and bacon," Zack said, pointing at the stove.

"Sure, I could eat," I said. "They look great. Did your mom teach you how to cook bacon and eggs?" I asked. The bacon looked terrific.

"No, it was my dad. He's a good cook," Amy said.

"Wait 'til you try them," Zack added.

I filled my plate, leaving plenty for the others. I sampled a slice of bacon. *Dang, the bacon is crispy, not hard or soft. It's just the way I like it.* I added ketchup to my eggs and mixed them up. Zack grabbed me a glass of milk. "This is good!" I nodded to Amy. "Thanks for the milk," I said to Zack.

Beth and Daniel were finally ready and joined us in the kitchen. "What's on everyone's agenda today?" I asked.

"We had talked about doing a little fishing, maybe a hike," Daniel said.

"Uncle Parker said his buddy was going to bring my car over. Other than a few minor dents and scratches, mechanically, everything is fine. I'll be happy to get my car back." Zack smiled.

"That's good. Parker said it looked a lot worse when he pulled it out of the woods," I said.

"What are you and Mom going to do today?" Daniel asked, changing the subject.

"Well," I hesitated and wrenched my lip, "we are going to try and find Jimmy's parents," I whispered.

"Why are you whispering?" Beth asked.

"I don't want Jimmy to know what we are up to," I said.

"Is he here?" Amy looked around the room.

"I don't think so, but you never know." I shrugged.

"I was thinking about visiting Grandma and Grandpa this afternoon. I think they will enjoy that," Zack said.

"I'm sure they will," I said, knowing I raised my boys right.

Sara strolled in and grabbed a plate, and I moved to the couch, giving her room to sit at the table to enjoy breakfast. Lexi and Claire were moments behind. I relaxed on the sofa, enjoying a quiet morning. I was startled when Claire sat next to me. "Mom wants to go with you today. Is that alright?" she asked.

"I don't see why not. The more the merrier." The question was not how many of us went; it was which house to start with. I would suggest the Blanchard location, only because it was ten miles away and Renovo was about thirty. But I was going to wait for the ladies to decide, so I wouldn't get blamed for going to the wrong location first. I had learned a lot over the past twenty-five years of marriage.

Sara startled me when she nudged me. I guessed I had drifted off. All my life, I've gotten little cat naps whenever the time presented itself. This was one of those moments. Sara, Lexi, and Claire were ready to embrace the day. We loaded up the car. When driving around locally, I didn't understand why we needed to bring a cooler. Maybe because we needed to refill our Pepsi—speaking of filling up, I needed to top off my gas tank before venturing out.

I was driving to allow the ladies more time to chat and strategize. Moments later, I pulled into the general store. The young man greeted us, and I asked him to fill it up. I walked inside and looked about. Not much had changed. The garage section was closed. I noticed a woman about my age working behind the counter.

"Hi, I'm John Malone." I nodded.

"I'm not selling the place," she said.

"What?" I was puzzled.

"I know who you are," she stated.

"I'm not here to buy the place. I only stopped to get some gas."

She looked me up and down, trying to get a read on me. "I'm not lying. I have no interest in owning a gas station slash general store," I said.

"That's what they all say."

"All?" I was puzzled. "Have others offered to buy this place?"

"Yes, all. I've had three offers to buy the place. I'll be clear: It's not for sale," she said forcefully.

"That's fine. Like I said, I'm not interested. I worked here as a kid. It brings back fond memories, but I have a life in Philly, and I'm not looking to move back to Lizardville."

She stared at me for a moment. "Alright, I believe ya." She gave a nod.

"So why is the garage closed?"

"Well." Her eyes lit up like a Christmas tree. I had touched a good nerve. "You see, I'm remodeling. The garage section is being converted to a hoagie shop." She smiled, pulling some blueprints from under the counter. She laid them on the counter. She pointed to a kitchen area, counter section, and four booths where people could enjoy their sandwiches. "It's been a dream of mine since I was a little girl."

"You're Sandy Peterson," I said joyously, pointing at her.

"Yes, you remembered."

"It took me a few minutes to make the connection. But, yes. I remember you from school."

"I always had a little crush on you back then. But you were already dating Sara. I'm glad it worked out for you," Sandy said, blushing. I could tell she meant that.

"Thanks." I nodded.

The door swung open, and the young man walked over. "That's thirty-five dollars, mister." I pulled out my wallet and handed him a credit card. He quickly passed it over to Sandy, and she processed the payment. "Would you like a receipt?"

"No, I'm good." I smiled. "It was nice seeing you again—best of luck with the hoagie shop addition. I can't wait to try one," I said as I returned to the car. I opened the door and slid behind the steering wheel. "Did you know that was Sandy Peterson?"

"Yes," Lexi giggled.

"What's so funny?"

"Did you know she had a crush on you in high school?" Sara said sharply.

"No, I didn't have a clue." I blushed, wishing I didn't have to be trapped in the car with them all day. I turned the key, and the engine roared to life. I focused on driving and keeping my attention on the road. In fifteen minutes, we could be interviewing Linda Brooker. I hoped to return early to spend time with my mom and dad.

"So that's it?" Lexi said anxiously. Sara giggled a bit, enjoying every minute of this awkward moment.

I twitched and wiggled a bit. I kept my eyes glued to the road. I could feel their eyes drilling into the back of my head. I hope they enjoyed torturing me. I slowed as we rolled into downtown Beech Creek. There wasn't much of a downtown. I drove past several businesses and then crossed the bridge. The small towns seemed to flow together. I glanced at the road sign that stated: "Welcome to Blanchard."

"What is the address?" I asked, hoping this would get the focus off me and some high school girl who had a crush on me.

"You'll turn right on Bald Eagle Lane," Sara said. Her head was down, eyes following the map on her phone.

I eased off the gas, looking right and left, reading each sign as they passed. Finally, I found the road and turned right. "What's next?" I quizzed.

"Go straight, about three streets, and you'll turn right. The third house on the left," Sara said.

I counted the streets in my head as we passed each one. I turned right, spotting the house. I inhaled, wondering how this conversation was going to go. *How do you tell someone they can see their son again: "I know he died thirty years ago, but I can summon him here."*

I pulled into the driveway. I placed the car in park and turned off the engine. I wiped my palms on my jeans before opening the car door. I gazed at the ladies; their facial expressions said it all. I took the lead as we approached the front door. I closed my eyes, inhaled, and pushed the doorbell.

I could hear the chimes inside the home. My mind was stressing out about what to say. *Maybe they are not home.* Then I heard footsteps approaching the door. My heart about jumped out of my chest when the door creaked open. I noticed the chain at the top for security.

"If you're looking for my son, I don't know where he is." Her voice quivered as if she was expecting trouble.

She and David had another child, or I have the wrong house. "Hello, we're not here for your son, ma'am." Our eyes met. "We're looking for Linda Brooker," I said nervously. *Get it together, John.* Sara stood next to me for comfort.

"You got the wrong house." She sounded relieved. "What do ya want with Linda?"

"Do you know her?" I asked.

"Do I know her? She's my sister." She sounded suspicious.

"I knew Linda a long time ago. I only wanted to say hello while I was in town," I said.

"I don't believe I caught your name," she said, the smell of alcohol heavy on her breath.

"It's John Malone," I said.

"It's not ringing a bell. I'll be sure to tell her you stopped by." She started to close the door.

"Wait! Can you tell me where she lives?" I asked sincerely.

"Last I know, she moved to Renovo." She met my eye again. "Can you tell we don't chat much?" She closed the door, and I heard her latch the lock on the door.

"That went well," I said, turning while I strolled to the car.

"That was a dead end," Lexi stated.

"Not really. We had a practice run, and we know she moved to Renovo," I said, smiling.

Sara smiled back. I turned the key and started our journey. I drove toward Lock Haven on Eagle Valley Road. We skirted Mill Hall, went through Flemington, and turned left on Fairview Road. I headed past Lock Haven University. It was a small college with five or six thousand students. I remembered a great pizza joint called the Snack Shack. Dad used to take Buck and me there when we were kids—best hoagies and pizza around.

I turned on Renovo Road. It skirted the Susquehanna River at the base of the mountain. The drive would take about thirty minutes. It was pretty this time of year. But I always preferred the fall colors. I continued north past Farrandsville. Some of these places looked just like I remembered them. It made me wonder if time was standing still. I continued north through the Bucktail State Park Natural Area. The woods engulfed us. I could catch a glimpse of the river here and there. We cleared the heavy forest. A sizeable vintage steel girder bridge appeared, soaring hundreds of feet over the Susquehanna River. I loved their humming sound as the tires rolled over the metal surface. The river now appeared to our left.

Five minutes later, the small town of Hyner flashed by. *I think the twenty homes that reside there won't mind us not stopping*, I chuckled to myself. Sara turned to me. "You alright?" I nodded and smiled.

I drove through Farwell and noticed the road sign that read, "Renovo: 3 miles."

"Do you have Linda and Dave's address?"

Sara turned, facing the front. She had been chatting with Lexi the entire time. I hoped they wouldn't ask me what they said. I wouldn't have the foggiest idea.

"You're going to stay on this road. It turns into Huron Avenue. Drive to the far end of town and look for Pine Street," Sara said.

I slowed. The large sign read, "Welcome to Renovo," and a picture of a large deer was painted on the left-hand side. The main street was lined with houses, not stores. This was a place time forgot. Or they forgot to change with the times. It was historic, to say the least. I drove by Yesterday's Restaurant and Hotel and several homes that had seen better days—past Big Louie's Pizza. I caught a whiff. It smelled pretty good. Maybe we could grab lunch on the way back. I continued farther by the Dollar General and Ma and Pa's Meat Market before returning to two-story homes that had to be a hundred years old.

"John," Sara yelled, "turn here!" She pointed toward the left.

I jammed the brakes while turning onto Pine Street. "What house number?"

"Number 384," Sara said, glaring at her phone.

I counted the numbers as we drove by each home. Their house was right on the corner. I could see the dike a hundred yards from the house. That barrier kept this house and this town safe from the mighty river. That sent shivers up and down my spine. I parked along the street. There were no driveways here. I turned the car off. I gazed at Sara and Lexi. "Let's do this," I said as I opened my door and headed down the sidewalk toward the front door. I stopped, waiting for the ladies to catch up. The three of us walked up together.

I didn't see a doorbell. I made a fist and lightly knocked on the door.

TWENTY-FIVE

We waited a few moments. Finally, we heard shuffling sounds inside the home, the lock was unlatched, and the doorknob turned. My heart raced as the door opened. I knew right away this was the Linda Brooker we were searching for. Without a doubt, this was Jimmy's mom. I remembered her facial lines and expressions. She staggered for a moment and stepped away from the door. I extended my hand for support. "Linda," I said softly as I entered the home.

"Johnny." Linda teared up and steadied herself against the wall. She looked like she had seen a ghost. *Oh gosh, wait until that happens.*

"I'm sorry to show up unannounced. Sara and I were in town, and I thought we might stop and say hello. How are you and Dave?" I asked.

Her mood changed rapidly from shock to anger. What had I said to upset her? Linda's face turned a few shades of red. She pivoted and walked into her living room. I followed, Sara and Lexi trailing a few steps behind. Linda abruptly stopped. "I don't remember inviting you into my home. Why are you still here?" she scolded me.

"I'm sorry to intrude. I didn't mean to upset you. Please accept our apologies," I begged. My eyes dropped, and my mouth wrinkled. She could see I was sincere. Linda lowered herself into a recliner facing the television. I took a seat on the couch closest to the recliner. Sara sat next to me, and Lexi took the final spot.

"Dave and I divorced a little over twenty years ago," Linda rambled, gazing at the TV. "After Jimmy passed away, everything changed. I never wanted to leave Lizardville. All our memories were there, including the ones with Jimmy," she sobbed. I picked up a box of tissues on the coffee table and extended them to Linda. She took a few and gave me a little smile. "Dave couldn't take it. He insisted we move, and we argued for days. I gave in for the sake of our marriage. Boy, was that a mistake." She shook her head with gritted teeth. "Well, I'll be nice and not call him names in front of you. Just know he's no good to me."

This is going to be a problem. How can we get Dave and Linda together to cross Jimmy over? My heart sank, knowing our last chance was slipping away. I turned my attention back to Linda.

"I'm sorry. Where are my manners? Would you all like something to drink? I have water, lemonade, even some iced tea," Linda asked, wiping tears from her eyes.

"We're fine, but thank you for asking," Sara and I said in unison.

"So, what made you come looking for me after all these years?" Linda sniffled. "How have you been, Johnny? Oh, did you know I read a few of your books? They are excellent. I always enjoy a good ghost story." Linda smiled.

This was going to be easier than I thought. I took Linda's cue. "Well, if you have the books here, I would love to sign them for you if you like," I offered.

"Oh my, signed by the author. Yes, please!" She stood and walked to the bookcase, pulling three books from the shelf. She opened a drawer, grabbed an ink pen, and laid it on the coffee table before me.

I gazed at the books, opened, personalized, signed each with a special note, and closed them. Linda smiled at me; I think I just made her day.

"It's an honor to sign these for you," I said.

"Oh, I can't wait to show the ladies at the bingo hall. I told them before I knew you."

"Do you have a cell phone by chance?"

"Why yes, I do." Linda smiled and handed me the phone as she straightened her hair with her fingers. "How do I look, dear?" She directed that question to Sara.

"You look amazing," Sara responded.

"Why, thank you." Linda smiled. I passed the phone to Sara, grabbed the books for Linda to hold, and scooched next to her, so Sara could take several pictures. Things were starting to look up. Now was the moment.

I sat, watching Linda read what I wrote in the books. She beamed with pride. "You mentioned you loved ghost stories. Do you remember Tom Evans and his mother Gladys? How about Old Man—" I stopped to correct myself, "I mean, Bob Smithers?"

"Of course I do. I knew them all. Gladys was an amazing person. She could see things before they happened. Did you know that? She could also talk to the dead. That's what the ladies used to say. I wanted to visit her to see if we could talk to Jimmy before he went to Heaven, but Dave refused, calling Gladys a witch and a con artist. I still regret that to this day. She passed away many years ago," Linda said.

She just made this conversation a lot easier. "I'm sorry, Linda. Where are my manners? Do you know Sara and Lexi?" I pointed to each of them.

"Of course, the Parker sisters. I used to play bingo with your mom. Did you know that?"

"Yes, ma'am, we remember," Lexi and Sara replied.

"You never answered my question, Johnny. What brings you here today?"

"Well," my heart was pounding heavily, "we stopped by to talk to you about Jimmy." Her expression changed, and her head tilted in interest. I went on to tell her about what happened the day Jimmy passed. I told her how he came back as a spirit and how Bob, Tom, and Gladys helped us cross over several spirits to the other side. Now, only Jimmy remained. I explained the ring Tom had left me and showed it to her. I told her that we thought if she and Dave could come to Lexi's house, I could summon Jimmy, they could get a chance to say goodbye, and Jimmy could finally rest in peace. Linda sat in silence after my long-winded story.

I wasn't sure if she believed me or not. I tried to get a read on her expressions, but that was impossible. I waited, not wanting to push or pry. It was Lexi who finally broke the silence.

"Linda, are you alright?" Lexi asked.

"I'm better than alright, dear. I've waited for this opportunity for thirty-five years. You can count me in. I can't wait to see my boy," Linda said, smiling while shedding tears of joy.

"How do we get Dave to show up?" I said point blank.

"That's not going to be easy. How long are you in town for?"

"Only a few more days. We plan to leave the day after Tom Evans' funeral services," I said.

"Oh my, I hadn't realized Tom passed away." Linda frowned. "He was a good man, cute too." She blushed. "Let me think… I have an idea." Linda stood. She walked briskly to the kitchen. I heard noises, cooking utensils, pots, pans, aww, heck, I wasn't sure what kinds of sounds they were, but there was a lot of commotion before Linda returned with some old letters, ink, pen, and paper. She opened the letters, one by one. She jotted down a phone number and then the address from the envelope.

"What are you thinking?" I asked.

"You mentioned Tom Evans' services. Tom and Dave knew each other very well. Even though Tom was older, they had a connection. Call him, or better yet, visit him and invite him to a celebration of life at your house. He'll show up. I would bet on that. I'll be there, and you can call Jimmy," Linda said, hands waving back and forth as she spoke.

"We can hold the event at my place," Lexi said.

"It just might work if he thinks this is for Tom," I said, rubbing my chin. *It's funny how you can devise a plan that seems to change without notice.*

"Oh, one more thing. I don't drive anymore. Can one of you come to pick me up?"

"Yes, I'll be happy to do that for you," Sara said without hesitation. Sara and Linda exchanged phone numbers. We sat and chatted about the good ole days for another hour before leaving.

I convinced Sara and Lexi to stop at Big Loui's Pizza for lunch. The place was tiny, but they had a few tables where we enjoyed lunch even though it was already midafternoon. No wonder I was hungry.

My mind worked overtime while driving back to Lexi's place. Dave Brooker lived in Sugar Valley. That was on the other side of the mountain—mainly farmlands. I wasn't sure how to get Dave to show up. I needed a backup plan but couldn't come up with anything at that moment.

I pulled into Lexi's quarter-mile-long driveway. I noticed only a handful of cars. If we were going to get Dave to believe that we were holding a celebration of life for Tom Evans, we would need more cars and trucks. I started counting Parker and his parents, Buck and Ryan, Claire and Lexi. Our vehicle and Zacks, but that was only eight. I'd have to work on that.

I stepped out. The house was quiet. We went inside to find the place empty. We piled back in the car and drove over to my parents' house. As I approached, I could see cars lining the long driveway. That was it. Scooter could also show up, and maybe some other friends could let us use their cars for a couple of hours. We were halfway to pulling this off. *Now, I only need to make sure Dave shows up!*

ZACK

TWENTY-SIX

Mom, Dad, and Lexi loaded up and headed out for the day. They had been gone over two hours, and it was apparent they would be awhile. That gave the rest of us time to explore. This time, we were going to be prepared for Jimmy. We filled up sandwich bags with salt and filled our pockets with protective stones. I think that's what Dad called them.

We tossed around a few ideas: visit the cemetery, stone quarry, or lumberyard. Ryan mentioned there was plenty of time to do all three. Claire, Amy, and Beth gathered supplies, packing them in an ice chest. I snatched a blanket from the hall closet. We decided to have lunch in the graveyard. That was enough to tilt my nerves, but I couldn't let the others know I was frightened. I smiled and agreed.

Ryan loaded a few flashlights and hand tools into a small backpack. I'm unsure what he was expecting, but we could never be too prepared. We loaded the car and ventured to the Lizardville Cemetery. The gates were open when we arrived. I guessed it was someone's job to open and close the gates daily. Ryan pulled down the narrow lane and circled the graveyard. We stopped near the rear of the new section where we buried Jimmy's remains. Everyone appeared to be tense. It was nice to know I wasn't the only one who felt this way. We walked over, spread out the blanket, and sat in a circle.

"Are we going to try and speak to the dead people?" Beth asked.

"I'm not sure that's wise," I said.

"Are ya scared?" Ryan pushed my arm, chuckled, and winked at Amy, who gave Ryan the cold shoulder.

"It's daylight. Do spirits come out in the middle of the day?" Daniel had my back. It was nice knowing my brother had taken my side.

"Haven't you learned anything yet? Spirits can't tell if it's night or day. It doesn't matter to them. They're dead!" Ryan shouted for effect.

We sat for over an hour, snacking on food and chatting about what it's like living in a big city versus a small town like this. They both had pros and cons. The girls ganged up, saying it would be better to find a midsize town. That would be the best of both worlds. Daniel and I both disagreed. Ryan was leaning more toward the girls' way of thinking.

Spending time in the cemetery was getting boring. We agreed to pack up and head over to check out the stone quarry. To our surprise, the place was packed with workers when we arrived. Trucks hauling rocks were going in and out. We could cross that off the list. We had the same results at the lumberyard. I wasn't sure what we were expecting. This was the middle of the week, and people were working.

Ryan backed the car up, and we headed to visit my grandparents. Ryan pointed to the home where Jimmy grew up.

"Wait!" Beth yelled. She pointed to the for-sale sign in the yard. The place looked empty. I wondered if Jimmy was chasing people away on purpose. I guess there was only one way to find out.

"Pull in," I said, pointing at the gravel driveway. "Let's check it out," I added, curious about what Jimmy's house looked like on the inside. Our parents played here, so why not?

"Now you're talking my language," Ryan said, backing the car up and pulling it into the driveway.

"What if someone sees us?" Amy said.

"They'll think we're looking to buy the home. No one will suspect anything," I said.

"I love it," Ryan said, turning off the car.

We sat in silence for five or six minutes. Before I decided to open my car door, there started a flurry of car doors opening. Ryan grabbed the backpack in case we needed light. We walked around the perimeter, checking for open doors or windows. I stepped on the front porch. I extended my hand and jiggled the doorknob. It was locked, too. I guess we could only peek through the windows. We took turns. I could see everything through the windows. The place was empty and looked dated—from the colors of the appliances down to the paneling on the walls. *Wow, no wonder this place is empty.*

We followed Ryan to the rear of the home—down a few steps to the cellar door. Amy hung tightly on my arm. Ryan twisted the knob. I felt relieved. The door was locked. Ryan turned, thrusting his body into the door. I watched as it flew open.

"See, it's not locked," Ryan said wryly. I watched him step inside. My curiosity was piqued at what lay beyond the door. I stepped forward, and Amy pulled me back.

"What are you doing? That's breaking and entering," Amy stressed.

"Not in Lizardville. Dad, Parker, and Buck know everyone. Besides, the place is abandoned." I watched Claire step around Amy and me. She vanished inside the home. Daniel and Beth nodded and went inside. Amy sighed, entering. She stopped briefly, tugging my arm. "Are you coming?"

I smiled and laughed. This was why I loved her. Ryan held his flashlight, handing one to Claire and Beth. "Sorry, I'm all out, and you were last to enter." Alright, everyone wanted to be funny. I got it. Amy and I tried not to stumble in the dark as we followed behind the others.

The basement was like many I had seen in the past—dark and empty with a strong mildew smell. There were a few boxes scattered about. But I highly doubted any of them belonged to Jimmy. We checked out the canning storage room and a coal bin for the furnace. But nothing I hadn't seen in the past. We followed the others upstairs to the main level. We didn't need flashlights to see. There was plenty of light shining through the windows. I remember Uncle Buck or Parker saying a new family lived here. But this place looked like it had been abandoned for many years. The floorboards creaked as we walked about. The kitchen was small with a bathroom to the left. There were two family rooms near the main entrance. Nothing but emptiness. Ryan nodded to the stairwell leading to the bedrooms. Maybe this would give us some insight into who Jimmy was. Perhaps it could even unlock the clue as to why he wouldn't cross over. Each step we took creaked or made some weird noise as we went upstairs. There was no sneaking around in this house late at night. A shiver traced down my spine.

The more oversized bedroom on the right would have been Jimmy's parents'. The room across the hallway must have been Jimmy's, or was it? I was surprised to learn they had an upstairs bathroom, which was cool. Most older homes only had one bathroom. I poked my head in Jimmy's room. Ryan was on the other side, looking out the window. I walked over to get a look at the view. I was amazed by the view of the lumberyard. No wonder Jimmy knew where to hide and all the escape routes. He could see how the place was laid out.

Daniel opened the closet door. It was small. He tapped around, looking for hidden compartments. Maybe we could pick up a few clues with a bit of luck. I gazed in the closet after Daniel moved on. My eyes focused on the lower baseboards. I even tapped the floorboards. Then I heard a thud instead of a thump. I backed up, retracing my taps. Same thing: thud. "Did you bring a flat-tip screwdriver?"

Moments later, Ryan placed one in my hand—a lump formed in my throat. I tapped around the board and then slid the flat end into a small gap between the boards. I forced the screwdriver down, then lifted it slightly. The board moved. I repeated the process until the board popped up. I began to shiver all over, and my teeth started to chatter. The temperature was dropping at a rapid rate.

"Guys!" Beth called out.

Ryan and I spun at the same time. Jimmy was blocking the doorway to the only exit we had. Jimmy looked upset. "We can explain," I said in a calm voice. I was amazed it was cold enough to see my breath in the air.

"What are you doing in my room?" Jimmy squinted, his face a deep shade of red. Jimmy gritted his teeth and clenched his fists. I had no idea what he was going to do. "I want you out of here now. That means now!" Jimmy hovered in front of the doorway.

I wanted to know what was hidden in the floor. "Cover me," I whispered. I turned, closing the door behind me. I dropped to my knees and pried the board off the floor. I glanced; it appeared empty. I shoved my hand inside, feeling around. My hand started to freeze. I jerked back. I was watching Jimmy float out of the hidden compartment. I was mostly sure the space was void of anything that would help us. I opened the closet door to find I was alone.

I heard screaming downstairs. I hurried to the door, flew down the steps, rounded the corner, and barreled to the basement stairwell. I hustled as fast as I could. I spotted Ryan heading out the basement door as it closed behind him. *Why would he do that?* Stunned, I stopped in my tracks. Jimmy stood, blocking my exit. I heard Ryan and Daniel pounding on the door from the outside, trying to force it open. They knew I was trapped. Jimmy had trapped me.

I pulled the bag of salt from my pocket and poured it into a circle around me. I held the stone before me. "Don't make me use this," I threatened Jimmy. I was unsure if it would do anything, let alone knew how to use it. I had the feeling that Jimmy didn't know if I could harm him, so he kept his distance. Yet he was still blocking my only way out. This was one of those moments when I wondered why I even came into this haunted house. I knew Jimmy lived here. I think he baited us. I was waiting for Jimmy to get farther from the basement door. I only wanted to leave.

"I'm sorry you live alone. I never meant to upset you. Please, Jimmy. Let me leave, and I'll never return," I said calmly.

Jimmy hovered in front of the door. The paleness returned to his cheeks. He eased his hands. He slowly drifted toward me, but still keeping the door jammed so the others couldn't enter. This was the final moment, my last stand. Jimmy moved in closer. "If you were not Johnny's son, I would possess you and end your life," Jimmy gritted through his teeth.

My heart fluttered, my head spun, and I wasn't sure what was happening. I tried to move, yet I couldn't. I'd never felt like this. My breath was short. The room spun as I watched Jimmy enter my body.

A sharp pain pierced my head. I closed my eyes, wondering if I was about to die. My knees buckled. That was the last thing I remember.

My eyes twitched and fluttered open, and my vision blurred. I saw Amy's face, and then Ryan and Claire crowded over me. "He's awake," Amy stuttered with a sigh of relief.

"What happened, dude?" Daniel questioned.

I coughed a time or two. "Water." My throat was dry like the desert sand. My sense of smell was gone; I could smell the mildew before. Now nothing. Ryan helped me sit up. My body was weak, arms heavy. Ryan and Daniel helped me to my feet. My legs wobbled, and I was unable to stand on my own. They carried me outside. The sun was bright as I closed my eyes. I understood they wanted me out of that house. Heck, I wanted to get out of the house.

"Can you tell us what happened?" Ryan begged.

"Jimmy," I managed to say. Beth showed up with bottled water. I leaned forward to gulp half the bottle.

"Easy, big boy," Ryan said, pulling the bottle away from my lips.

I inhaled. The warmth of the sun felt refreshing. I wiggled my fingers and toes. My senses were slowly restored. I rested a few more minutes before we walked to the car. Everyone was anxious to know what happened. The best I could explain was Jimmy passed through me, sending my body into shock. The next thing I remembered, everyone stood over me, asking what happened.

We relaxed in the car for another ten minutes before visiting our grandparents. I never realized that Daniel and I were just like Mom and Dad: Ghosthunters. I suggested we keep this between the six of us. Everyone agreed. I hoped they would all stay true to their word.

JOHN

TWENTY-SEVEN

The three of us walked inside the house. Mom was excited to see Sara and me. Much to our surprise, Sara's mom was here, too. "The boys are out back playing horseshoes with your dad and Sara's dad," Mom said.

Buck was the first to ask while the others watched them tossing the horseshoes. "How did the trip go?"

"Better than expected! Linda's on board for sure. We have one little wrinkle. Dave and Linda are divorced," I said as Buck's jaw dropped.

"Where does that leave us? With only one parent, will it work?" Buck asked.

"We have a plan." I explained everything to Buck, who agreed. We felt confident this was going to work. Right now, I only wanted to put this behind me and enjoy the rest of the day with my family. Tomorrow would be another day.

Morning snuck up on us. Once again, I had slept longer than expected. I could get used to this. I rolled over, noticing Sara still sleeping. I checked my phone for missed calls or messages. Sometimes, the publisher would have questions or need me to do things for them. I only had one message; it was from Linda. It read that the girls at the Bingo Hall were jealous that she had gotten me to sign her books. Now, they all wanted to buy my book and get it signed. I smiled, knowing I would have to please my new fans. It was almost 9:00. It was time to get out of bed and be productive.

I smelled bacon the second I opened the door. I knew I was putting on some weight this week, but there was too much food and not enough willpower to say no. I readied myself for the day. I went to the kitchen, hoping the bacon was gone. But it was not. I grabbed one slice and avoided the eggs. I was proud of myself. The boys and girls were still sleeping in the tent outside. I wasn't surprised. They had a ton of fun with the family yesterday.

If we could send Jimmy to the other side, maybe my next trip would be fun and relaxing. I wanted to see if anyone wanted to visit Penn's Cave. That would give us something to do today. I had planned on calling Dave Brooker because it might alarm him if we drove to his house to invite him to a celebration of life.

I heard Sara stirring in the hallway. I made her a cup of coffee so she could sit and relax. That was what vacations were for. Of course, this had been anything but relaxing. I let the ladies chat around the table as I leaned back on the sofa. I pulled the slip of paper from my pocket and unfolded it, wondering when would be the best time to call Dave. I took a deep breath, finished my coffee, pulled my phone out, and dialed his number.

The phone started to ring, and by the third ring, I figured he wouldn't answer. I waited for the message to start but was pleasantly surprised when I heard his voice. "Hello, this is John Malone. Is this Dave Brooker?"

"Yes," he replied.

"The one who lived in Lizardville a little over thirty years ago?" I needed to make sure I had the right Dave. His confirmation brought a smile to my face. "Do you remember Tom Evans?"

"Of course, he owned the gas station and general store. Oh, Johnny, you worked for Tom, didn't you?" Dave asked.

"Yes, I did. I wish I were reaching out with better news. Tom passed away several days ago, and several others and I are in town for a limited amount of time. We were wondering if you would like to join us for Tom's celebration of life?"

There was a long silence.

Did I lose Dave? Did my phone stop working? I checked a few things before asking, "Dave, are you there?"

"Yes, I'm here. I am sorry to hear of Tom's passing. I knew Tom but not like some of his other customers, and it has been a long time." Dave was looking for an excuse.

"Dave, it would mean the world to me if you would show up," I said, hoping that was all it would take.

"Well, Lizardville brings back bad memories. I hope you understand." Dave searched for a way out.

"None of that was Tom's fault. This place holds good and bad memories for all of us. But I understand. I'll let the other customers know you couldn't make it."

"I didn't say that, exactly." Dave paused. "So when is it?"

"Tomorrow. It starts around seven." I gave him Lexi's address.

"Who's all coming?"

"I don't have all the names handy, but the list keeps growing. We all loved Tom," I said, hoping he would agree to come.

"I suppose I can make it. Is there going to be food?" Dave asked.

"What kind of celebration doesn't have food?"

"I'll see you tomorrow at Bob Smithers' house," Dave said, and he hung up the phone.

I was stunned. Dave knew Bob Smithers' address. Was he aware that Bob passed away a few years ago? Oh gosh, what if he didn't? This was going to be another surprise for Dave. I only hoped he was going to keep his word and show up.

We needed to inform Linda everything was set, order food, and get plenty of cars to fake a large party.

The day slipped away quickly, and we made all the arrangements immediately. Lexi wasn't the happiest, complaining that I could have given her two days to pull this off. We were exhausted and hit the sack early to rest well for the big day.

I woke early, just before the sun rose. I heard noises coming from the kitchen. I was blown away when I entered the kitchen to find Zack and Amy preparing breakfast for everyone. I jumped in to help. The more hands, the better.

Helping had its perks. That meant we were the first to eat since the others were still sleeping. It also gave Zack and me a little time to chat.

"Do you think this is going to work?" Zack asked.

"You mean sending Jimmy to the other side?" I whispered.

"Yes, that, and stop whispering," Zack snickered.

"You never know. Jimmy could be listening," I said, my eyes focused and unblinking.

Zack laughed and walked away. I guess I was sounding a little crazy. It wasn't long before the others were awake. Parker and Ryan showed up in separate cars. Buck was the last to arrive. We went over our assignments. Every role was crucial. Sara was going to pick up Linda. Lexi, Amy, and Beth would care for food and set things up at the house. Parker, Buck, and Ryan would shuttle cars back and forth. Zack, Daniel, and I had shopping details. *Why do I always get stuck with shopping?*

Finally, the boys and I headed to the store. I checked off each item on the list. I bought more plastic bags, salt, candles, and even incense. There was a small store on the outskirts of town inside an elderly woman's house that Lexi had told me about. She was excited to see us. She noticed my ring and admired it. She even offered to help us with our mission. I declined, hoping I would not regret that later. We grabbed a few more protective stones for safe measure. The last stop was the grocery store.

I decided to pick up extra food. Since we had been eating Lexi's food all week, it was the right thing to do. The cart filled up quickly. The boys tossed in a few family-sized bags of Middleswarth Barbeque potato chips. I loved them growing up. Sara and I decided to stop eating so much junk food a few years ago. This week was an exception. It was a family vacation. So, I told the boys to toss in a few more bags. *Just in case, you know.* We loaded up on Pepsi, bacon and eggs, hamburgers and hotdogs, and even chicken and steaks. Why not live it up? We only had two days left.

I rounded the corner, and it was much to my surprise. "Hello, Scooter," I said.

"Oh my gosh!" He was just as surprised as I was. I started to introduce the boys to him. They reminded me he was at the party the other day.

I filled Scooter in, from finding Jimmy's remains, placing them in the cemetery, and all the other events that had happened. He was saddened to learn of Tom's passing. He invited himself to join us this evening to witness Jimmy crossing over. The more, the merrier, and we all welcomed him to join.

"I'll see you in a few hours," I said, giving Scooter a fist bump. The old gang was coming back together for one final hoorah.

"I wouldn't miss this for the world," Scooter replied.

I double-checked everything on the list, making sure not to miss anything. I even quickly called Sara to make sure nothing else was needed. My next call was to the Snack Shack Pizza joint. I order several large pizzas for lunch. I knew I was hungry, and I'm sure the boys were too.

I slowed, pulling into the driveway. Wow, there were several cars I didn't recognize. Where had Parker come up with the extra cars?

"Oh, oh, no," Zack hollered. "Check out my car!" he yelled excitedly.

My head tilted, and my eyebrows raised. Parker had pulled off another miracle. His buddy at the shop had fixed the dents and given the car a new paint job.

Zack jumped from the car the minute I parked it and ran over to see. Parker beamed with pride as he handed the keys back to Zack. "You are the best uncle ever," Zack cried with joy.

"I hope it was worth the wait. Besides, it wasn't all me; it was your Uncle Buck's idea, and most of the money came from him and your father," Parker said.

I was lost. I don't remember saying I was going to help pay. Buck and Parker felt terrible, just as Sara and I did over Zack's car. But would they help pay? That was another issue. I guess I would have to talk to Sara about it later. If my memory served me right, Buck still owed me money from the last time I was in town.

Zack and Daniel danced around the car. At the same time, Beth and Amy were excited for Zack. That left me to unload the vehicle. Thank goodness for my nephew Ryan, who came to my rescue. After the groceries were put away, we huddled together to polish off the pizza, leaving only a few slices for leftovers. I sat on the couch, trying to get a power nap before all the fun started.

TWENTY-EIGHT

The nap was just what I needed. I felt refreshed and ready for the challenge. It was time to get this show on the road. Sara took the car and headed to Renovo to pick up Linda Brooker. Jimmy was going to be surprised to see his mother. I felt confident I could make him appear. I wasn't sure Dave Brooker was going to show up. Everything depended on Dave. I didn't have a backup plan. Most of the time, we didn't, but with the stakes being this high, I should probably think of one.

I wanted to call him to confirm, but that might alarm him that something was off. I thought about having Buck or Parker standing by to pound on his door and drag him out of the house. I believed they called that kidnapping. None of us wanted to go to jail over this. I'd keep my fingers crossed and hope for the best.

Two hours passed. I thought Sara would have been back by now. I sent her a text, but she hadn't responded. I stared at the clock, watching the minutes tick by. I felt a hand touch my shoulder. "Relax, Dad," Daniel said. "Mom will be back shortly," he added.

I hugged him. He was right. I had nothing to worry about. At that moment, I was glad Lexi had a gravel driveway. I heard a car come to a stop and shut off its engine. I leaned over the couch. It was Sara. A sigh of relief filled me. Linda stepped out of the passenger's side door. Wow, she was wearing a long, elegant black dress. Her makeup and hair were done up, and the little black hat was the icing on the cake. *Man, she looks fabulous for her age.* Maybe she was trying to impress Dave and let him know what he had lost. If I were Dave, I would take notice.

That's when it hit me: none of us were dressed up. This was supposed to be a celebration of life. Most people attending would be dressed up. I told the others. Beth, Amy, and Claire said they would change into dresses. Buck and Parker shook their heads. I'd take that as a no. I went to the bedroom, opened my suitcase, put on a dress shirt, tucked it in and added a belt. Not bad for the last minute. Zack and Daniel followed my lead.

Sara entered with Linda beside her. She gazed around the room, noticing we had all changed clothes. "I'll be right back," Sara said, heading straight for the bedroom.

"Hi Linda, thank you for coming," I said, extending my hand. She pulled me in tight for a hug.

"I have to admit I'm nervous and excited," Linda said, wearing a mile-wide smile. "I'm excited to see Jimmy and nervous about seeing Dave." She grimaced.

"You look amazing. You have nothing to worry about," I said.

Sara entered wearing a lovely black dress. I smiled and gave her a wink. Lexi walked in wearing black. This was starting to fit the occasion. All we needed was for Dave to show up, and we could get this show started. I heard a car door slam. My heart skipped a beat. This was it. "Places, everyone!" I yelled.

Linda turned her back to the door, pretending to talk with Sara and Lexi, just in time, as someone knocked on the door. Everyone mingled. I looked around. The place looked perfect. I was turning the knob and pushing the door open. I smiled. "Oh, hey, Scooter," I said.

"Don't act so disappointed," Scooter said.

"Sorry, I thought you were Dave," I said. I watched Linda mingle. We might not have to hide her in the bedroom. That might work if she kept her back to the door until Dave entered. I still wasn't sure how to tell Dave we had asked him here to summon Jimmy so he could say goodbye. I'd play that by ear. Maybe Linda could help with that.

Scooter walked around. He was surprised to see Linda follow through and show up. The clock was ticking. Dave was already twenty minutes late. I was beginning to worry. The sun had set. Lexi turned on all the outside lights. I paced back and forth. Thank goodness Lexi had hardwood floors. Sara stopped me and handed me a plate of food. I tried to push it away, but Sara insisted. *Happy wife, happy life*. I smiled and took a bite of the sandwich she had prepared for me. Five minutes later, I whispered thank you in her ear as I tossed the empty plate into the garbage bin.

It was a little after 8:00. Dave was almost two hours late. It was apparent he wasn't going to show. Then I heard brakes screeching. Someone was here. I walked to the cur-tains, pulled them back, and noticed Dave stepping out of his truck. My heart skipped a beat.

"He's here," I announced. Linda dashed back and forth, asking the ladies if she looked alright. She looked fine. I wasn't sure what all the fuss was about. Lexi set the large picture frame containing Tom's picture in the center of the table to show that's why we were all gathered.

The doorbell chimed. I was impressed by someone who knew how to use the doorbell. I waltzed over and opened the door. "Hi, I'm John Malone," I said, extending my hand.

Dave grabbed my hand. He had a firm grip. He wore blue jeans, a black dress shirt, and a sports jacket. I was surprised. "I'm Dave Brooker. I used to live on Lizardville Road many years ago. Sorry, I'm late," Dave said. "Traffic," he joked.

"Welcome, there are still plenty of folks here. Several have come and gone already," I lied. I noticed Zack giving me the evil eye. I taught my children never to lie. But this was a unique circumstance. "There's food and drinks over there." I pointed to the table and counter. I noticed Linda still had her back to Dave. That was good. Parker and Buck stepped up and introduced themselves. He seemed to remember us. I caught his smile when he eyed the food. I closed the door and flipped the lock switch. Dave was not going anywhere.

Everything was going as planned. Dave had been here ten minutes and had yet to notice Linda. Lexi blocked his view, followed by Claire, Beth, and Amy. Sara and I intro-duced Dave to our boys. "It's a pleasure to meet you, Mr. Brooker," Zack said.

"Oh, please call me Dave," he said as he finished putting food on his plate. Dave mingled and then found a place to sit and eat. We chatted a little more until Dave finished his food. Dave walked into the kitchen to place his plate in the garbage. He noticed the woman wearing a lovely black dress that almost covered her ankles. The dress was flattering and her figure divine. Long silver hair cascaded past her shoulders. I watched, waiting for the fireworks to start.

"Hello, I'm Dave. I don't believe we've met," he said, extending his hand.

Linda giggled and then slowly turned around. Dave took a step back. "Linda?"

"Hi, Dave." Her hands trembled slightly. She looked down to avoid eye contact.

"Wow, you look amazing," Dave said. He bit his lip, not sure if he should believe what he was seeing.

The room fell silent. All eyes were on the two of them. Dave seemed happy to see Linda, and she was delighted to see him. This was going better than expected.

"I didn't realize you knew Tom Evans," he said.

"Only when I would stop at the store. He was a nice man and very polite." Linda smiled.

"That sounds like Tom," he replied.

I didn't want to push things, but we needed to get this show on the road. "Can I have everyone's attention?" I looked about the room. "Please take your seats. I want to say a few words about Tom." Everyone shuffled about, taking any open chair. Dave ushered Linda to the couch. This was working perfectly. I hope it stayed that way.

Lexi dimmed the lights. At the same time, Sara and Claire lit candles. Dave was still unaware of what was taking place. I needed to make sure Dave and Linda each held a protective stone. Beth handed each of them one and placed a small bag of salt before them. Dave looked puzzled but went along with things. I didn't think he ever got over losing Linda. Maybe we were about to play matchmaker.

Lexi dimmed the lights a little more. The candles flickered, casting the illusion of dancers on the wall. "We're here tonight to celebrate Tom Evans. He touched all of us in one way or another." I paused. Dave was still okay. "As many of you know, Tom and his mother Gladys believed in the supernatural. The spirit world," I said as a light breeze whipped through the house, sending a chill in the air. "Whether you believe it or not, this is what Tom requested in his last will and testament." I held up an envelope and waved it around. Little did Dave know, there was nothing inside except for blank paper. I focused on Dave, who wrinkled his nose and lip, yet remained calm.

"Tom requested we call out to him tonight," I said. I watched Linda place her hand on Dave's thigh to take his mind off what I said. "Tom, we call you here tonight to say your final goodbyes. We invite you to join us." I repeated this several times. My nerves were steady while waiting for Tom to appear. The temperature dropped five, maybe ten degrees in seconds. I noticed Dave shivering, and he glanced at Linda, who nodded in approval.

The lights flickered. The wind whipped, dousing a few of the candles. "Tom, we invite you here as our friend. To all the people we have lost: Gladys, Bob, Jimmy," I calmly said. I was keeping one eye on Dave, who didn't appear to have heard me. I repeated this several times. Linda gripped Dave's hand and whispered something to him. It looked like he wanted to leave but remained to please Linda.

Several lights twinkled in the middle of the room about six feet from the floor. One, two, three, ghostly images formed: Bob Smithers, Gladys Evans, and then finally Tom. Dave's mouth dropped, his lips quivered, and he pushed himself back into the couch. Linda was fascintated. She bit her lip with anticipation. She waited for her son to arrive.

Tom smiled. He floated about, happy to see so many faces gathered for him. "Thank you," he said, smiling. "I'm no longer in pain. I feel alive again."

"You all had better not make a mess in my house," Bob scolded us as he floated around, inspecting what he still considered his home.

"Bob," Gladys said. Bob bowed his head. It only took one word from Gladys to hush Bob.

"We invite one more spirit to join us. Jimmy, please show yourself. We invite you here," I requested.

Dave quickly realized what we were doing and whom I had invited. He started to stand. Linda never let go of his hand and pulled him back down to the sofa. Dave appeared confused. His hands shook, and his eyes fluttered. Gladys took Bob and Tom's hands, forming a small circle. She chanted something in a language I didn't understand. A new set of lights twinkled within the circle. I continued to invite Jimmy. Everyone started holding hands. A small figure pooled together. The lights flashed and danced about, and finally, Jimmy had arrived.

Tears began to flow from Linda's eyes. Dave draped his arm around her shoulder for comfort and reassurance. Jimmy's translucent body glowed before us. He was upset and obviously not happy to be in our presence. "I warned you once, twice. This time, you're going to pay!" Jimmy's anger grew, his face turning a light shade of crimson.

He spun in a circle, glancing at each of us and pausing before me. "Johnny, I warned you." Jimmy bared his teeth. "Tonight, I'm taking one of your boys," he spat.

The wind whirled as Jimmy took flight, blowing out the rest of the candles. Lexi's quick reaction saved us from darkness when she flicked on the flashlight on her phone. Buck and Parker followed her lead. Jimmy darted in a circle, passing through Bob and then Tom, rendering them unconscious as their spirits slumped and sank to the floor. Gladys raised her hand, only a second too late as Jimmy barreled through her midsection. I watched as Gladys's translucent figure draped over the table.

Jimmy was too powerful and very much in control—the room filled with a dense fog, casting us into blindness. "I warned you all," Jimmy yelled, as I covered my ears from his deafening voice.

Sara pulled herself close to me, begging me to stop this before someone got hurt or worse. I couldn't see anything. I felt my knees shaking, and for the first time, I feared we had bitten off more than we could chew. My body shivered. The temperature was almost freezing. I could only imagine what the others felt: my boys, Amy, Beth, and Claire. They must be terrified. I turned my attention to my hand, mainly my ring finger. I balled it into a fist. I was willing to use the ring's power to end Jimmy's curse. "Please put an end to this madness," I whispered. I then repeated myself. It wasn't working. I wasn't sure what I was thinking. I'm not a wizard. I have no training. I've always been lucky that Tom, Bob, and Gladys were able to help us. I looked upward. I needed a Hail Mary, as they say in the sports world. "Annabelle, can you help us?" I begged a few more times. I had no idea if she would be able to return or if she would even help us after we crossed her over.

Jimmy's thunderous laughter dropped me to my knees. He was enjoying himself, having a blast toying with us. I think we had finally pushed Jimmy to the breaking point. He continued to laugh while the fog thickened. The room was getting colder by the second. Jimmy was going to kill us all. This was not the way I wanted to die.

"Boy, don't make me take you behind the woodshed!" Dave hollered. "I'll give you a whooping like you won't forget," Dave huffed and puffed. Jimmy stopped, and the room fell silent. This was the longest thirty seconds of my life.

The fog subsided. Lexi cast her light toward Dave and Linda. They were the reason we were here. We needed to give them the chance to say goodbye.

"Stop it, Dave. We lost him once, and I won't lose him again," Linda said resolutely. I could see her breath in the air. Linda appeared brave and possibly ashamed that her boy wanted to take another life.

Jimmy's eyes blinked, frozen in time. His mouth hung open, eyes growing wider by the second. "Mom," he whimpered. He glanced to her left. "Dad." Jimmy was stunned. His parents were both there to witness his rampage. "What are you doing here?" Jimmy spoke softly. Tears tracked down his pale cheeks. Jimmy's body glowed. He softened, surprised his mom and dad were sitting together on the couch. A warm feeling flooded his body. His cheeks turned a light shade of red.

Tom, Bob, and Gladys regained their strength and floated upward, resting along the wall. They were allowing Jimmy the time and space he needed.

I could hear a pin drop. Linda whimpered, "It's really you." She couldn't believe what she saw with her own eyes. "We never got to say goodbye. I never had a chance to tell you how much you meant to me. I loved you from the day you were born. I remember the first time I held you. I knew you were special." Linda paused, cupping her hand over her mouth, and began crying.

"Mom, please don't cry, please!" Jimmy begged.

"My love has grown over the years. Not a day goes by that I don't think of you. I miss you more than you will ever imagine," Linda sobbed.

Jimmy made eye contact with his dad. "I missed you both," he said, drifting closer to his mother and father.

"We missed you, too," Dave said, choking the words out. Dave and Linda gripped each other's hands, not wanting to let go. I sat in amazement, looking around the room to make sure everyone was alright. All eyes were on Jimmy, Linda, and Dave.

"Why did you leave me?" Jimmy diverted his eyes to the floor. He was speaking in a passive tone.

"We never left you," Dave replied.

"You moved away?" Jimmy trembled. His lips quivered. "I was scared and all alone." Jimmy cried a river. His face distorted, making several odd shapes.

"We were hurting so much that we couldn't bear living in that house," Linda cried. She extended the palm of her hand toward Jimmy's cheek. He drifted closer.

"I blamed myself for your death. I was not the father you deserved. I wish I would have spent more time with you. I was too focused on myself and my work. I tried to be a good provider." Dave wiped the tears from his eyes. "I'm so sorry, son. I'm sorry I wasn't the father you deserved.

I'm sorry we moved away. I'm sorry for everything." Dave broke down and whimpered.

"I stayed in the house. I waited, wanting you to return. I wanted to show you I was still here. I chased everyone who tried to buy the house away. Yet no one came to visit. Only you." Jimmy pointed to Zack and Daniel. "None of you ever came to see me either." Jimmy frowned, looking at me and the rest of the original group."Why not? I thought we were friends."

That was new. Sara and I glanced at each other. Our eyes were swollen and overrun with tears. I shook my head.

"When did you two go to Jimmy's house?" Sara questioned the boys.

"Not now. We'll tell you later." Zack turned his attention back to Jimmy, Linda, and Dave. I would definitely revisit that later.

"It was more pain than we could bear. To go back to your home would have pushed me over the edge. We were only kids," I said.

"I felt deserted, unloved." Jimmy shook his head.

"Your dad and I love you more every day. I know we are both proud of you for waiting for us to come and see you. I'm sorry it took this long. Thank you for waiting." Linda grimaced, knowing it was time to say goodbye. She extended her palm again. She was lightly brushing Jimmy's cheek. "Oh, it's cold!" She pulled back.

"I'm sorry, Mom," Jimmy said, puffing his cheeks, turning them a light shade of pink.

Linda tried again. "That's better, dear." Linda stayed strong. "I love you, Jimmy," she said, then pulled her hand back. Jimmy's entire body blushed.

"I love you too, Mom." Jimmy's eyes darted back and forth from his mom to his dad.

"I love you too, Jimmy," Dave said softly.

"Thank you for coming back for me," Jimmy said. He drifted toward the ceiling and then smiled at each of us as if saying goodbye for the last time. His eyes locked on his mother and father as he mouthed the words, "I love you."

Jimmy appeared confused. He faded in and out. Then, slowly, his fingers started to evaporate. Then, his arms, feet, and legs began disintegrating into small particles and drifting upward. Lastly, his body and smile were gone like dust in the wind.

Linda broke down in tears. Dave wrapped his arms around her for comfort as he pulled her tight. Sara and I sat in amazement. It was painful yet beautiful in many ways. Jimmy had crossed over, just as we had hoped he would.

I glanced at the far wall. Tom was breaking down and drifting upward. He managed to mouth the word, *"bye,"* just before he vanished. Bob was the next one to go. He mentioned for Lexi to take good care of his house. Finally, Bob was going to be with his family. I felt happy for him.

"You've done well, my son." You made Tom and me extremely happy. You earned the ring. I'm proud of Tom for choosing you to continue the family tradition," Gladys said as she started to break down and drift upward. "Study the manuals Tom left you!" She smiled, waved, and blinked out.

TWENTY-NINE

We sat in disbelief. Our plan had worked. Jimmy was finally at peace. Tom, Bob, and Gladys could now rest. Everything had gone as planned. Every ghost I knew was in a better place. I glanced at the large ring on my finger. I decided to take the ring off and place it in the safe at home. I never wanted to see another ghost as long as I lived.

Dave was reluctant at first to believe what he had witnessed, insisting this was all some hi-tech computer thing we set up. Linda promised him it was not. The two of them chatted and talked about what we had just watched. Dave had another plate of food. And of course, so did Parker.

We informed Linda and Dave that we had found Jimmy's remains at the dam. We explained we tried to cross him over by placing his body in front of the tombstone made for Jimmy. They were thankful and knew that when they visited his gravesite, his remains would be there.

Upon learning that Sara needed to drive Linda home, Dave stepped forward without hesitation, offering his assistance. As Dave and Linda embraced, gratitude radiated from their every word, expressing heartfelt thanks for our support, especially in enduring Jimmy's antics. I guessed everything was ending the way it was supposed to.

As I awoke the following day, a serene tranquility filled the air. The disturbing energy seemed to have dissipated, leaving Lexi's home in a state of peacefulness. *Perhaps*, I thought, *the valley can finally find solace*. Pride swelled within me as I reflected on my family's unity and resilience. Together, we embarked on the journey to bring closure to this chapter of our lives, united in one purpose and determination.

We attended Tom's official celebration of life at the funeral home. It was a lovely service. A few dozen people stopped by to say goodbye to Tom. It made sense. The longer a person lived, the fewer people would attend the funeral because most of their friends were already gone.

We paid our respects. I was hoping for one final appearance from Tom. But once a ghost crosses over, there's no coming back.

I also had another idea I wasn't sure how to present to Sara. I wanted to buy the home that Jimmy grew up in. We could fix it up, giving us a place to stay when we came into town. Then, we wouldn't have to be a burden to any of our family, and we would still be close. I wasn't sure about staying next to a lumberyard. They can be pretty noisy.

On our final night of vacation, we finally held our fish fry. Buck and Parker showed the boys how to grill up the fish they had caught all week. While waiting for dinner, I cast a line in the creek at Lexi's and enjoyed a little fishing with my father. These were the memories I would cherish forever.

Zack waited patiently until everyone had settled around the picnic tables and finished their meals. I watched Zack approach Amy with a determined stride, a glint of nervous excitement in his eyes. I knew he was up to something, but it was only a feeling.

Kneeling before her, he produced a small box from his pocket. His heart must have been pounding with anticipation. I heard him ask Amy for her hand in marriage. Amy's gaze flickered between Zack, Sara, and me, her hesitation fleeting before she finally said, "YES!"

ACKNOWLEDGMENTS

I'm a writer, so I primarily work alone. I greatly appreciate my wife, Toni, for tolerating and putting up with my weird ways and allowing me the time I needed to complete this story. Thank you for being the first to read my work and giving me valuable feedback.

Thank you to 4 Horsemen Publications, Erika Lance, and Valerie Willis for taking a chance on me and allowing me to follow my dreams.

Thank you to Gayle Staggemeyer for finding those elusive mistakes that drive readers up the wall, along with your thoughts and suggestions during editing. I valued all your suggestions, ideas, and criticism throughout the writing process.

A shout-out to Autumn Skye for the brilliant cover art and typesetting you created for this story.

Thank you to all the Alpha readers—Silvia Curry, Carolyn Hornick, Jessica Altier, and Teresa Allaert Thompson—for taking the time to read my story and tell me what worked and what didn't.

A special shout-out and thank you to all the readers for your support. I could not do this if it were not for you. You are the best.

BOOK CLUB QUESTIONS

1. Would you go on a ghost hunt with John and Sara?

2. Would you want to read another book by this author?

3. Did you guess the ending? If so, at what point?

4. Which twist surprised you the most?

5. If you could ask the author anything, what would it be?

6. How does the book's title work with the book's contents? What would you choose if you could give the book a new title?

7. Would you ever consider rereading it? Why or why not?

8. Are there lingering questions from the book you're still thinking about?

9. Did the book frighten you or get under your skin in any way?

10. Which characters did you like best? Which did you like least?

11. Who would you choose if you had to trade places with one character?

12. What did you think of the book's length? If it's too long, what would you cut? If too short, what would you add?

13. What songs does this book make you think of? Create a book group playlist together!

14. Which places in the book would you most like to visit?

15. Did the book strike you as original?

16. What do you think of the book's cover? How well does it convey what the book is about?

17. What other books by this author have you read? How did they compare to this book?

18. Was the pacing—beginning, middle, and end— done well?

AUTHOR BIO

Steve Altier is a bestselling paranormal, mystery, and suspense writer. He is known for his multi-award-winning series, *The Lizardville Ghost Stories*, and *Lizardville Side Stories* series. Steve grew up in a small town in central Pennsylvania. His parents owned the damkeeper's house on Lizardville Road. Across the street was an old, broken-down dam and the remnants of the ax factory.

Steve and his buddies spent many days exploring the abandoned factory. Unexplained things happened when

Steve was a child—inspiring his love for everything spooky and many of his stories. Steve lives in Florida with his wife, four daughters, and four cats.

Learn more about Steve and his work by following him on social media or visiting his website. **www.stevealtier.com**

Steve would love to hear from you. You can email him at **authorstevealtier@outlook.com**

Discover more at
4HorsemenPublications.com

10% off using HORSEMEN10

www.ingramcontent.com/pod-product-compliance
Lightning Source LLC
Chambersburg PA
CBHW020148310726

48970CB00006B/2062